COMING HOME

When Maddy Green, new vicar of Llyn Ddu, meets the land-owning Collett-Evans family she falls for charming Tristan and dislikes sullen Ben. But all is not as it seems. As Maddy battles opposition in the parish and tries to help troubled teenager Chloe, secrets are revealed leading to the downfall of one brother and the redemption of another, a suicide attempt and breaking of a curse. Ultimately, will Maddy find love and a place to belong?

SUSAN SARAPUK

◆

COMING
HOME

Complete and Unabridged

LINFORD
Leicester

First published in Great Britain in 2009

First Linford Edition
published 2010

British Library CIP Data

Sarapuk, Susan.
    Coming home. - -
(Linford romance library)
1. Women clergy- -Fiction. 2. Landowners- -
Fiction. 3. Wales- -Fiction. 4. Love stories.
5. Large type books.
I. Title II. Series
823.9'2–dc22   **20292724**

ISBN 978–1–44480–492–8

Published by
F. A. Thorpe (Publishing)
Anstey, Leicestershire

Set by Words & Graphics Ltd.
Anstey, Leicestershire
Printed and bound in Great Britain by
T. J. International Ltd., Padstow, Cornwall

This book is printed on acid-free paper

1

The candles flickered in the draught and the bronze cross on the altar glowed in their warm light as Maddy Green knelt before the bishop and the registrar said the final words that would make her the new vicar of the parish of Llyn Ddu.

She was taking charge of four ancient churches set in the crook of the Welsh mountains around the rim of the lake from which the parish took its name, and in the few weeks since she'd got the job she'd often wondered what she was letting herself in for. After all, her last church, Saint Martin's, had been in a bustling urban parish with a large congregation and lots of activities. Maybe if it hadn't been for Michael she might have stayed.

She firmly put that thought out of her head as she surveyed her new congregation. Saint David's was a small church, with black pews and beams and bare stone walls. It was packed this evening with worshippers from all the other churches — she suspected it would be fairly empty on Sunday with only a few farms dotted around the lake and a row of cottages at the top of the lane.

What would these people think of her — an outsider who didn't speak the language and a woman? Malcolm, their last vicar, had been here for years and had become an established part of the community. She'd heard that nobody had wanted to take on the parish and was beginning to wonder what was wrong with it.

Once the service was over everyone retired to the hall across the lane where the women of the parish had laid on a spread.

'We're so glad you're here vicar!' Maisie Rees, one of her churchwardens gushed.

'Oh, call me Maddy.'

Ken Williams, her other warden delivered a heartwarming speech of welcome when everyone had eaten their fill and then it was Maddy's turn to speak. 'This is going to be a new challenge for me,' she said. 'And for you too.' There were a few nods around the room. 'I hope that together we can grow our Christian community here. I will certainly devote my time and abilities to serving you.'

Bishop Wyn was one of the first to leave. Carrying his case with his robes and bishop's crook, he took Maddy aside.

'I wish you the best,' he said formally. 'If there are any problems you know where I am.' But the tone of his voice was less than encouraging.

'Thank you, Bishop.' She shook his hand. She hadn't even met him until this evening and when he'd smiled a greeting, the smile hadn't reached his eyes. She sensed a degree of ambivalence in him.

'Hi, I'm Ros Lannigan. Welcome to

Llyn Ddu,' Maddy turned away from the departing bishop to find a young woman, about her age, with red curly hair and a freckled face at her side. 'We're glad to have a new vicar at last, but, speaking personally, I'm even happier that you're a woman. Now we can set an example to all these men!'

Maddy laughed. She liked Ros immediately.

'And these are my boys!'

Maddy stepped back as two young boys came crashing past, playing a game of chase.

'Josh, Ethan, say hello to the new vicar.'

'Hello, Vicar,' they chorused.

'Twins,' Maddy stated the obvious and they both pulled a face as if to say they didn't particularly want to be.

'Handy for playing the same part in the nativity.' Ros laughed. 'My husband, Tim, runs the farm just along the lake. You must come by to visit with us very soon.'

Not everyone was as welcoming;

Maddy couldn't help overhearing a conversation between a man and a couple of women.

'Slip of a girl. She looks far too young. Where's she come from? What's she done?'

'Quite right Cecil. Anyway, I don't agree with women priests.'

'Did you notice who was missing tonight? Without the Collett-Evans' support, well . . .'

People were beginning to drift away. There was the sound of car engines starting up. By ten o'clock it was all over and the lights were being turned off in the hall.

'I wonder if it's a sign, the Collett-Evans not being here,' Maddy overheard one of the ladies who'd been washing up say.

But by that stage she was too tired to ask who the Collett-Evans were and merely called out goodnight before heading for the vicarage next to the church — her new home for the next few years, she hoped.

Although she'd moved into the vicarage over a week ago Maddy never failed to be astounded by the silence when she woke up in the mornings. In the city she'd been used to the constant rumble of traffic and police sirens going off at all hours of the night. Here the silence engulfed her.

She lay in bed, watching the autumn sunshine streaking the far wall, picking out the silver strands in the wallpaper and after a while she could hear the gentle swish of the breeze in the pines in the churchyard, the caw of the rooks and the distant suck of the lake lapping through the reeds and onto the red-soiled shore.

There was little time to loiter. She made toast and tea, eating and drinking quickly before making her way over to the church. It looked picturesque with its solid tower, ancient lychgate and small graveyard. The lane petered out at the lake's edge just beyond the cemetery wall. Maddy wandered down to the water to watch the mist slowly lifting from the surface. She'd already seen boats sailing on the lake on a clear day.

Then, glancing at her watch, she hurried into the church, the door clunking heavily as she unlocked it. Inside there was an ethereal silence. Maddy lit the candles before ringing the bell. She wasn't really expecting anyone to join her for morning prayer, but just as she reached her stall and was opening her book to begin, Ken Williams strolled in.

'Morning, Vicar.' He picked up a prayer book and sat in the choir stall opposite her. Maddy returned the greeting, glad to have someone to share the daily office with.

When their prayers were over she put out the candles and then pulled out her diary.

'Who do you think I should visit first, Ken?' She clicked her pen, ready to write.

'Well, you've already called on Maisie and me,' he leaned back against the choir stall. 'I'd start on your housebound. Eira Penry, up at Talycoppa farm, she's been a great worker over the years but can't get out anymore . . . '

Maddy scribbled as he made suggestions.

'And who are the Collett-Evans?' she finally asked as his recommendations dried up. 'I heard people mentioning them last night, commenting that they weren't there.'

'Ah.' Ken sighed. 'Have you noticed the big house at the very top of the lane, by chance?'

Of course she had. It was unmissable with its long driveway and turrets and gables overlooking a long sweep of lawn down to the edge of the lake. The plaque on the imposing gate read, *Collett Hall*.

'The Collett-Evans have been the squires around here for centuries. They endowed the church when it was first built five hundred years ago, and they're still big financial contributors.'

'So why weren't they at the induction last night? Are they against women priests?'

Ken Williams closed his prayer book and studied it in his hands. 'I don't know,' he said.

Maddy thought he sounded cagey but she didn't press him.

'Well perhaps I ought to pay a visit.'

'You can try.'

Maddy didn't know what that meant. She watched as Ken replaced the prayer book on the table at the back of the church.

'Will you be here every morning?' she asked.

'I try to get here when I can.' He picked up his hat where he'd left it next to the pile of books. 'I certainly didn't want you to be alone on your first morning. I didn't know whether you'd be spooked.'

'Spooked?' Maddy frowned.

'Malcolm died in the vicar's stall, one morning when he was about to say morning prayer. Carys Evans definitely heard him ring the church bell. I found him later that morning when I came to check a baptism register, on his knees, keeled over, face down on the open prayer book.'

'Oh, I didn't know about that. I just heard that it was a heart attack.'

'He was a good man,' Ken said wistfully.

'Thanks for being so thoughtful.' Maddy smiled. 'But it doesn't spook me. Don't worry about it.'

'I'll be off then.' He placed his hat on his head. 'I've got to take the wife into Wryton. See you tomorrow morning, Vicar.'

Maddy checked the church one more time then locked up after her. When she came out into the graveyard Ken Williams' car was gone and the rooks were cawing in the pine trees.

2

Maddy spent the day visiting and getting to know the country lanes of her new parish. Late in the afternoon she was on her way back to the vicarage when she saw the sign for Lannigan's Farm and, remembering her invitation from Ros, she turned in, her little red car clattering over the cattle grid and down a mucky lane. She pulled up in front of a grey stone house.

Ros came out of one of the outhouses, wiping her hands in an apron, her hair tied back in a scarf.

'Hi!' She looked delighted to have a visitor. 'I didn't expect a visit so soon. I'm honoured. I'm well down the pecking order you know.'

'I was passing.'

'I've just finished firing,' Ros said. 'Come in, I'll make us some tea.'

'Firing?'

'Yes, I'm a potter as well as a farmer's wife.'

Maddy followed her into a generous kitchen with an Aga and a huge oak table. An elderly dog, lying in a basket, raised its head to see who the visitor was before laying down again.

'That's Jess,' said Ros. 'Her walking days are over I'm afraid. The others are out with Tim up at Maes Coch at the moment. And the boys will be home from school in half an hour.'

Maddy didn't want to keep her but it was hard to resist the warm fire, comfy chairs and the big slab of ginger cake that came with the tea. She discovered that Ros was an outsider too.

'I met Tim when I was exhibiting at a country show ten years ago,' Ros said. 'And then it was a case of we had to get married if you know what I mean.'

'And have you fitted in?'

'It took me a while, but Tim's family is an old one, been here for generations. I'm accepted now and I love it here. You will too, I'm sure,' Ros said reassuringly, adding, 'So what's your background, then?'

Maddy told her about the Cambridge degree, the early career in marketing before she had a religious experience whilst doing charity work abroad during her summer holiday.

'So I trained for the ministry and within two years I was running Saint Martin's. Very successfully if I may say so.'

'If it's not too intrusive a question, what made you want to leave?' Ros sat forward in her chair, cradling her mug in her hands. Maddy could see that her nails were dirty with clay.

'Relationship problems,' Maddy shrugged. 'Well, partly that. I'll tell you all about it sometime.'

'Sure.' Ros smiled easily.

The door banged open and Josh and Ethan burst in.

'Mum! Mum! He's got my maths book and won't give it back!' one of them cried — Maddy couldn't tell which was which.

'I'll be on my way then,' she said, putting the mug down on the table. 'Thanks for the tea and chat.'

'Come again.' Ros was reaching for her boys to separate them. 'And if you need anything don't hesitate to ask. I'm always around.'

★ ★ ★

Relationship problems. Maddy couldn't help thinking about Michael as she drove away. When he'd first appeared in Saint Martin's she hadn't thought of him in any other way than being a godsend to the new music group she was trying to establish. He was a superb guitarist — and so he should have been for he spent his working life as a recording session musician. It was only as the group really took off under his leadership and started attracting young worshippers that she began to see him in a different light, unwillingly, for she'd always vowed not to mix work and her social life. Getting involved with someone in the parish was not a good idea.

But there seemed to be a mutual attraction — they couldn't help flirting during their weekly meeting to discuss the music for the following Sunday — and eventually, when he'd asked her to a gig he was playing, she'd said yes.

It was surprising how much they had in common spiritually, which was the most important thing to her. With the ratio of available Christian men to women not being particularly favourable she'd never dreamed she'd ever find someone so 'normal'. And then, of course, Sophie had come along and all those dreams had collapsed.

No, don't think of it! She told herself sternly. Saint Martin's was in the past and she was here now, with a new life and new people to meet. And what a glorious place this was, what a place to live!

Maddy turned on the radio. Classic FM was playing *The Banks Of Green Willow* by George Butterworth — one of her favourites — the hedgerows were bursting with fat red hawthorn berries and far below the calm lake reflected a blue sky. She couldn't ask for better.

Suddenly she saw a four wheel drive coming straight towards her. Quickly Maddy turned the steering wheel to tuck into the side of the road, realising too late that there was a ditch. She felt the car squelch into mud on one side.

'Rats!' Carefully she pumped the accelerator but the wheels spun around uselessly. She was stuck! Then she noticed that the Range Rover had stopped alongside her and the driver had wound down his window. She cut the radio and opened hers too.

'Are you all right?' the young man asked. He had dark, unruly hair falling to his shoulders and was wearing a frayed work shirt and shabby Barbour jacket.

'I'm stuck,' she wailed.

His dark eyes surveyed her, seeming to alight on her clerical collar.

'I'm Maddy, the new vicar,' she

16

answered his gaze.

'Yes, I can see that,' he said coolly. 'You're obviously not a country girl or you'd know you can't tuck into these hedgerows and that's no car for driving along country lanes either.'

'Well, if you hadn't shoved me off the road . . . '

'Wait a minute,' he cut into her. 'I'll turn around just up ahead and pull you out.'

Before she could say anything he drove off again. Maddy sat back in her seat and waited, trying to work out whether to be offended by his manner or glad that at least she had someone to help her.

Two minutes later he was back, drawing up just ahead of her. She watched as he jumped out and pulled a tow rope from the back of his vehicle before bending down in the ditch to attach it to her car. She thought she at least ought to get out.

'I'm sorry if I've inconvenienced you,' she said flatly, watching him knot

17

the rope with capable hands. She saw that the cuffs of his shirt were frayed too. Probably a local farmer struggling to get by. Maybe he'd been in church last night although she couldn't recall seeing him and she probably would have noticed a handsome young man because there were so few of them around.

'My fault,' he said gruffly. 'I suppose I did take up most of the lane.'

He couldn't know, of course, that she'd been distracted by the view of the lake and thoughts of Michael and had swerved without thinking.

'Right, that ought to do it.' He tugged on the rope. 'Let's try it.'

She climbed back into the car and waited until she felt the pull of the larger vehicle in front. Gradually and without any fuss her car was pulled from the ditch and back to the security of the road.

The young man came back to retrieve his rope.

'Thank you,' Maddy waved as she

poked her head out of the window. 'I don't know who you are.'

'Ben,' he said before turning away and climbing back into his car.

A bit abrupt, Maddy thought; maybe some of the locals weren't that keen on getting to know her. He pulled in half a mile ahead to let her pass. She waved her thanks again and drove straight home.

3

After morning prayer the following day at which she was once again joined by Ken Williams and an hour in the study sorting through paperwork, Maddy decided that the first visit of her day should be to the Collett-Evans. As it was a crisp autumn morning and Collett Hall was only at the top of the lane Maddy walked the short distance.

The imposing gates stood open which seemed to suggest there was a welcome. The driveway was open too with well clipped shrubs affording a view stretching down to the lake in one direction and the house in the other.

On the forecourt in front of the house gleamed a silver car, the sort that looked Italian and expensive. The Virginia creeper caressing the warm stonework of the house's façade was flaming crimson.

She rang the doorbell and waited, looking up at the gables and latticed windows. Presently the door opened revealing an older woman dressed in an aproned uniform.

'Oh . . . em . . . hello . . . I'm . . . ' Maddy began somewhat hesitantly.

'You're the new vicar,' the woman said.

'Yes, I've come to pay a visit.'

'I'm Rita Teague, the housekeeper. Do come in.'

Maddy followed her across a chequered hallway with a grand oak staircase and paintings of men she assumed to be the squires through the ages frowning down sombrely at her from the dark panelled walls.

'Will you wait in here? I'll bring some tea, shall I?'

Maddy wasn't sure she'd be here long enough for tea after the whispers she'd overheard the other night, but then she knew how to fight people who had a prejudice against female clergy and she wasn't going to dodge a confrontation.

Better to deal with it right at the beginning and show she wasn't going to be intimidated by anyone.

She was admiring the view down to the lake when she heard footsteps behind her. 'Lovely isn't it?'

Maddy swung around to see a man standing in the doorway.

'Of course, when you've grown up with it as I have you can get a little jaded. Hello, I'm Tristan Collett-Evans.' He came towards her, extending his hand.

'I'm Maddy, Maddy Green, the new vicar.'

He was handsome, clean-shaven, dark hair styled neatly, affable blue eyes and a mouth with a hint of laziness that made her almost forget herself. When she clasped his hand he held it a fraction longer than a formal handshake warranted.

'Delighted to meet you. Sorry I didn't make it the other night. There were reasons, partly because I've only recently come down from London . . . But never mind, another time. Ah Rita . . .

tea, good. Please sit down, Vicar.'

'Call me Maddy.'

'I quite like calling you vicar.' His eyes twinkled. 'It's a bit of a novelty because you're a woman. Bit of a change from Malcolm.'

Maddy sat down on a green velvet sofa. This wasn't what she'd expected at all. She took the tea from the house-keeper and observed Tristan Collett-Evans as he accepted his. He was dressed in an expensive suit and she could smell his aftershave from here — something understated and exotic.

'How are you settling in? Tell me a bit about yourself,' he said.

Usually Maddy was the one to ask the questions, but he was very good at teasing things out of her.

'And what about you?' she said finally, when her cup was almost empty. 'I hear your family have lived on this land for generations.'

'That's right. Henry Tudor granted us lands for supporting his claim to the throne. We've a long and complicated history, too much to share today because I'm sure you've got other people to visit. Some other time perhaps, if you'd like to . . . ' His piercing eyes invited agreement.

'I'd love to,' Maddy gushed then checked herself. She was a professional, and this was an impartial visit to a parishioner. 'I know your family has strong connections to the church too and I'd like to hear all about that some day.'

'Some more fortuitous than others.' The smile faded. He was looking over her shoulder. Something outside had caught his attention. Maddy followed his gaze as she rose from the sofa, just in time to see the man who had helped her yesterday, with his sleeves rolled up, pushing a wheelbarrow across the gravel.

'That's the man who gave me a tow yesterday,' she said, 'I'm afraid I got mired in a ditch.'

'Really,' Tristan Collett-Evans didn't sound that interested. 'That's Ben, he likes to make himself useful around the place.'

Tristan walked her to the door.

'Thanks for calling,' he said as they paused on the steps. 'You're the sort of vicar who might just manage to entice me back to church.'

As he was speaking Ben came around the corner of the house and stopped as he saw her.

'Hi.' Maddy raised her hand in greeting.

He merely gave her a curt nod in response, exchanged a look she couldn't fathom with Tristan, then continued pushing his wheelbarrow onto the lawn in the direction of the trees a hundred yards away.

Even his rudeness couldn't spoil Maddy's good mood as she wandered back to the vicarage. So what if the gardener didn't like her? Tristan Collett-Evans seemed to. Now if only she could persuade him back to church — what a coup that would be! What a great start to her ministry that would be!

It was only later, as she was driving back from a visit to the organist at Saint

Non's on the other side of the lake that she realised he had told her nothing about his family. Was he alone in that big house? What about parents, siblings?

Ah well, she reflected with a smile, that would give her a good excuse for another visit!

★　★　★

There was a good turnout in all the churches on Maddy's first Sunday — even the tiny Saint Stephen's in the middle of nowhere had a congregation of a dozen for the communion service late in the afternoon.

The main service was held in Saint David's. Here there was even a choir — albeit a very small one, consisting of three older ladies, an elderly man who warbled the tenor line, one child and — amazingly, Maddy thought — a young teenage girl who also doubled up as the server.

Maddy was disappointed to see that Tristan Collett-Evans wasn't in the family pew in the front. Ros was in the row behind though, smiling encouragement. Maddy thought her sermon was a blinder and she had a number of favourable comments afterwards. Then Cecil Pugh, the church treasurer, a large man in his sixties still sporting a full head of hair and wearing a suit with a waistcoat, accosted her.

'Now, Vicar, the church council meeting on Thursday — I've got a few items for the agenda,' he pulled a piece of paper from his waistcoat.

Maddy glanced at the list. 'I'm sure that if time allows we'll get around to discussing them,' she said. 'I've got a few things myself.'

'Humph!' he stabbed a finger at her. 'I hope you're not going to be one of those feminists who think they know best and won't listen to anyone else, because in this parish we know how to speak up!'

Before she could respond he walked away.

'I'd like to say don't worry about

Cecil,' Ros said at her shoulder. 'But he likes to be in charge. He used to be the county surveyor before he took early retirement.'

'Well forewarned is forearmed.'

'Great sermon by the way.'

★   ★   ★

The teenage girl was one of the last left in church when Maddy came out of the vestry after disrobing. She was diligently tidying up the books in the choirstalls.

'Thanks for your help,' Maddy said. 'It's Chloe isn't it?'

'Chloe Carson,' the girl nodded. She was very slender in that gawky teenage way and looked pale. Her blonde hair was tied casually in plaits either side of her head, like a child.

'How old are you Chloe?'

'Fourteen.'

'Which school are you at?'

'The comp in Wryton.'

'I'm hoping to visit the head there

28

soon to arrange to come in for assembly. Where do you live?'

'The other side of the lake. Dad owns the boat rentals.'

'Oh, I see . . . so you don't go to Saint Non's over there, then?'

'I like this church better,' Chloe's green eyes were adamant. 'Besides, I like to help here.'

'Oh I'll find plenty for you to do,' Maddy warned. She'd always tried to encourage young people in church.

Chloe smiled eagerly and it lit up her face.

'Do you want me to carry your robes for you?' she asked.

'I'll manage.' Maddy almost felt sorry when the girl's face fell.

Ken Williams came out of the vestry at that point.

'Ready, Chloe?' he said.

'Yes,' came the diffident reply.

When Maddy went out of church she saw Chloe climbing into the church-warden's car for a lift home. Maddy waved as she walked past but Chloe was slumped in the passenger seat, a sad look on her face.

Her dad owned the boating business across the lake; maybe she ought to pay him a visit.

★　★　★

But all thoughts of that went out of her mind as she prepared for the first parish council meeting. Inevitably people were going to want to get things off their chest, but she had her vision to communicate, too.

They met in the church hall on a Thursday night, twenty two of them all looking towards her expectantly. Alright, she'd proved she could take some services; now could she lead when it came to buildings and money and all the practical things that made up the running of a parish?

'Right,' Maddy said briskly, getting down to business after the prayers. 'Let me tell you about my vision for the parish. I noticed we had some young

30

people in Saint David's on Sunday morning; I want to develop some Sunday school and youth work. There must be lots of youngsters in the local villages looking for a place to go.'

She saw Ros nodding her head enthusiastically.

'And I want to do something about the music. The organ's fine,' Maddy nodded at the elderly Klara Robinson, 'but we're never going to have a cathedral quality choir and I think that if we had some more musical instruments . . .'

'Lord help us! I hope you're not going to bring guitars into the church!' Emlyn Thomas cried.

'We are a traditional country church,' Cecil Pugh agreed.

'But we have to move with the times,' Maddy reminded them. 'Young people look for something different.'

'You want to be very careful, Vicar. You certainly don't want to lose any of the people you've already got here,' Cecil Pugh chided her.

Maddy knew they would have this discussion. As they talked it became clear that the council was fairly evenly divided. Then Ken Williams spoke up.

'I think we should give the vicar a chance,' he said. 'Malcolm was good to us but the parish has been declining over the past few years. If she can do something to bring more people in at the very least we ought to let her try.'

There were rumbles of assent. At least her churchwarden was on her side and Ken carried a lot of weight in the parish. Maddy felt relieved.

Then Cecil Pugh cleared his throat, gearing up for another attack.

'I think we need to remember whose money keeps this place going,' he reminded them. 'Saint Non's needs its roof repairing, there's dry rot in Saint David's and the graveyard is unsafe. And we're going to be short of our quota payment the next quarter. You might have all these big plans, Vicar, but we don't have the money, and we won't be giving it either if we're not happy.'

Maddy sat back and listened as a heated discussion erupted.

'I'm just saying,' Cecil Pugh spread his hands. 'You all know how friendly I am with the Collett-Evans. If they don't like it we could lose their sizeable financial contribution.' He turned defiant eyes on Maddy. 'You can't just walk in here and do as you like.'

The battle lines were drawn. But as she got ready for bed that night, listening to the high wind in the pines, Maddy decided that the best thing she could do was to ignore Cecil Pugh. If she had to get by without money then she would, she would pray for it! There were more important things than buildings and graveyards and quota payments.

★   ★   ★

The following day Maddy drove to the other side of the lake. Down a short lane off the main road was a mobile home and a large shed and a red notice that read *Boats For Hire*.

She was getting out of the car when she saw a man dressed in overalls coming up from the water's edge. 'Mr Carson?'

'Yes, I'm Lucas Carson.' He set aside the part he'd been rubbing with a rag on a colourful boat parked on a trailer. 'You must be the new vicar. Sorry I can't shake your hand, but I'm a bit oily at the moment. Do you want to come in?'

She followed him into the caravan. Inside it looked just like a house.

'I'm afraid I'm not too good with visitors,' he apologised as he invited her to sit down.

Maddy looked around; the room was functional with few feminine touches — some lace curtains at the windows and a floral lampshade.

'I met Chloe the other day. She was very helpful in church.'

'Aye, she seems to live in that place.'

Lucas Carson grimaced. 'She's at that awkward age.'

Maddy wanted to say that church was a normal thing to do but didn't.

'I don't see much of her these days. She's in her room or out somewhere. Since her mother left . . .'

'Oh?' Maddy's ears pricked up.

'Reckon it's all right to tell you, you're the vicar after all.'

Maddy tapped her nose to signal it was in confidence.

'Lyn left me nearly eighteen months ago. Moved away to the Lake District with her new man. I don't know what to do with Chloe half the time now she's a teenager. She needs a mother around really, or a sister. Listen, can I get you something to drink?'

'You're a busy man and I don't want to keep you,' Maddy declined.

'Won't be busy for much longer,' he sat down on a green and brown patterned sofa. 'No boats in the winter, or not enough business to justify opening. And we had such a bad summer this year.'

'Times are tough,' Maddy commiserated.

'And the ground rent is going up again. If I have another bad season next year . . . ' He shrugged. 'Why am I bothering you with all this?'

Maddy could see then how Chloe had a lot of uncertainty in her life.

'I'm glad Chloe's going to church,' Lucas Carson said. 'At least she's getting involved somewhere, not hanging around and up to no good. Does she have any friends there?'

'Well I've only been there one Sunday so far so it's hard to tell,' Maddy stalled. 'But I'm planning on getting some youngsters in.'

Lucas nodded. 'It'll do her good. There's nothing much around here for her. Can't expect her to be interested in the business.'

By the time Maddy left him she had a better understanding of Chloe and the look of utter despair and sadness she'd seen on the teenager's face as

Ken Williams had given her a lift home. It was not an easy time for her or her father. He seemed like a good man, struggling to do his best and she felt sorry for him.

When Maddy got back at the end of a day's visiting she made straight for the church to say evening prayer. She was surprised to find Chloe waiting for her in the porch. 'Chloe, how did you get here?' She didn't exactly sound welcoming.

'I rowed across the lake,' came the answer. 'I thought maybe I could do the service with you?'

Maddy let her light the candles and do the readings from the Bible. Afterwards she felt honour bound to ask her back to the vicarage even though she was longing to check her messages and then kick back.

'I paid your father a little visit today, Chloe,' she said as she served them toast and tea.

'Yeah,' she said indifferently.

'I like him.'

37

'He's okay.'

Maddy watched the teenager spread jam on her toast then proceed to nibble around the edges. She asked her about school and friends and life at the lakeside, and generally got non-commital answers.

'Do you think God punishes people?' the teenager suddenly said.

'In what way?'

'Like, for the bad things they've done.'

'Well I believe in ultimate judgement,' Maddy began but was immediately interrupted.

'There's a tale about this church and the lake, did you know? There was a young girl, over three hundred years ago. Letty Pendle was her name. They say the squire got her pregnant and then accused her of being a witch. The vicar at the time conspired with him and they had her drowned in the lake, just down the lane here. Some people say there's a curse on the place now; that's why Malcolm died so suddenly in the church. I hear the previous vicar had to leave because of ill health. The Collet-Evans always seem to escape though.' She glowered at her nibbled toast.

'That's a strange story,' Maddy said carefully.

'I hope you'll be all right!' Chloe looked at her fervently. 'I think you will be because you're a woman. I hate the Collett-Evans though. My dad tries to shield me but I know, I see the letters; they're putting the rent up for the business and I don't think we'll be able to pay it. It's just not fair is it?'

'Lots of things aren't fair.' Maddy shook her head.

Chloe suddenly glanced towards the window.

'It'll be dark soon, I'd better get back.' She got up from her chair.

'Let me drive you home.'

'No, I'll be fine. I've done this loads of times.' Chloe assured. 'Thanks for the tea and toast. Would it be all right if I came again?'

Maddy walked her down to the edge of the lake where a boat was tethered to a post among the reeds. There was a very short jetty with some of its slats missing. She watched the teenager climb in and cast off, a look of concentration on her face as she began to row smoothly out into the calm lake.

What a strange story, she thought as she returned to the vicarage to the accompaniment of rooks arguing in the trees. Back in the kitchen she noticed that Chloe had only eaten half a slice of toast.

An hour later, having looked up the number in the database, she phoned to make sure Chloe had arrived back safely. It was Chloe who answered and she sounded overwhelmed that some-one had cared enough to check.

4

Maddy set her plans into action straight away. She visited the local primary school and the comprehensive in Wryton and asked Chloe to marshall some young people together for a special service. Then she assembled a group of musicians and together they began to work on some new music.

That first Sunday at Saint David's she used a modern language version of the service and a piano, guitar, violin and two flutes. A few eyebrows were raised, and Cecil Pugh glowered at her throughout the whole service. His response to the changes was to chatter loudly at the back of the church afterwards saying how terrible it was that they were allowing those 'happy clappies' into their church.

'We're going to have a youth service at Christmas,' Maddy announced within his hearing. With an exasperated splutter he turned on his heel and stormed out of church.

'Do you think you might be changing things a bit too quickly, Vicar?' Ken asked kindly.

'Change or die Ken,' she said wryly. 'Change or die.'

She'd heard no more from Tristan Collett-Evans since their first meeting, despite his promise to come to church, and she often found herself thinking of him as she drove past Collett Hall every day.

One day, when she was in Wryton on a busy market day and walking towards the newsagents, she heard a familiar voice. 'Vicar!'

Maddy stopped suddenly on hearing the voice and turned to find that Tristan Collett-Evans was standing just a few yards behind her.

'Hello there,' he called after her, smiling and catching up to her.

'I haven't seen you in church,' was the first thing that came to mind.

'Ooh, sharp,' he held up his hands.

'I'm sorry.' Now why did she say that?

'No, you're quite right.' He laughed. 'I did say I would come. But I've been in London on business. Am I forgiven?'

'Well as a vicar I have to forgive you!' He grinned.

'I'm meeting a colleague for lunch soon,' he looked at his watch, 'but have you got time for a coffee?'

Maddy found herself saying yes. He led the way across the square to The Duke, the grand Georgian hotel facing the war memorial. He was obviously known there because the waiter greeted him by name and showed them to a table by the window.

'How are you getting on?' he asked as the waitress delivered two Americanos in expensive china cups with complimentary German biscuits on the side.

'I think I'm surviving,' Maddy picked up a packet of sugar and shook it before tearing off the top and emptying the contents into her coffee.

Tristan sat back easily in his chair, one arm extended along the window ledge. Just as on their first meeting he was dressed in a suit and smelled of expensive aftershave. Not the sort of man she usually liked, yet there was something about him — maybe it was the affable eyes and that mouth which gave him a 'devil may care' air. It was refreshing to someone who for the last few years had had to carry the weight of parish responsibilities on her shoulders.

'It's very parochial here,' he said. 'But that's country life for you.'

'What business do you have in London?' Maddy was determined that this time she was going to be the gleaner of information.

'I dabble in investment — property mostly. I couldn't stay here permanently, I need to get up to the city. What about you, are you a country girl?'

'Not until now,' Maddy sipped her coffee. She felt warm inside. 'But I like it here already.'

'Well when you've lived here all your life . . . ' one hand smoothed his lemon tie. 'Actually, they have a nice little scene going here on a Saturday night. All the young professionals for miles around come into town. You should try it sometime.'

'I'm afraid that Saturday's not good,' Maddy said. 'Sunday's my busiest day, you see, so I usually always try to get an early night.'

'Ah, occupational hazard.' He grimaced and stirred his coffee. 'Now, pardon my asking, but no partner?'

Maddy shook her head. Tristan Collett-Evans raised an eyebrow as if he was surprised.

'It's not easy being a vicar's wife.' She smiled. 'What about you?' If he could be direct so could she.

'Not currently,' he answered before he was distracted. Maddy followed his gaze to see a man about the same age dressed in a dark wool coat and carrying a briefcase weaving his way towards them.

'This must be your lunch appointment,' she said.

'Andrew, meet the new vicar.' Tristan rose from his chair.

The man shook hands with her.

'Have you got him into church yet?' he said. Maddy didn't like the way he sounded.

'Not yet!' Tristan stepped in quickly.

'Well,' she said, pulling her bag off the back of the chair. 'I'd better be going. Nice to meet you, Andrew.'

'Call up at the house anytime,' Tristan invited as she was leaving. 'I'd love to see you again.'

'Come and see me.' She laughed. 'On Sunday in church!'

★　★　★

There was a path that led out of the creaking gate at the back of the churchyard and along the edge of the lake. How far it went Maddy didn't know but she thought she would find out. She'd been sitting at her desk and mulling over Sunday's sermon for far too long and really needed to clear her head.

Water slurped amongst the reeds. Ducks bobbed on the water, dipping their heads to hunt for flies and tiny fish. Across the lake the majestic mountains rose to the sky, their lower slopes dotted with farms. Somewhere in the distance a tractor droned.

Maddy negotiated the muddy path framed with hawthorn and blackberry bushes, wondering if it would be possible to walk all the way around on a day when she had time, of course, for the perimeter must have been five miles in circumference. As she was contemplating this a barrier loomed up ahead, a wooden fence with no style.

It was climbable, she assessed, and before she'd had time to think about it she'd put one foot on a wooden slat and swung her leg over, dropping down on the other side. Rhododendron bushes obscured the lake. Maddy pushed her way through them gradually emerging

47

in a clearing at the water's edge. Glancing to her right she suddenly realised where she was as the sloping lawn afforded an unimpeded view of the gables of Collett Hall. Private property! Too late she realised she was not alone and had been seen.

Ben-with-no-surname had been tying up a small boat at a jetty. He might not have seen her if she'd retreated quickly except for the labrador that jumped out of the boat and lolloped over to her side. At least the dog seemed friendly, its tongue hanging out, eager to lick her.

'Hab!' Ben called out, turning as he did, a fishing rod in one hand and a large plastic cooler box in the other. He froze when he saw her.

'Miss Green,' he said coldly. 'This is private property.'

'Yes, I realise that now. I'm sorry,' Maddy held out her hand to the dog who licked it enthusiastically. 'I started to walk around the lake . . .'

'And fences mean nothing to you?'

'Well . . . ' She flushed with embarrassment, then recovered herself; it was an honest mistake after all. 'There was no sign. I didn't know I was coming onto the estate. I'll leave.'

'You need to acquaint yourself with the country code, Vicar.' He whistled and the dog trotted back to his side, tail wagging. 'You can't just climb over a fence when you fancy. There are rights of way.'

'I'll remember that next time,' she said coolly, stung by his school teacher attitude. Who was he after all? The gardener, the groundskeeper — whatever. 'Maybe I'll ask Mr Collett-Evans if I can have permission to cross his land. I'd like to walk around the lake.'

'You do that,' came the cynical comment.

'He seems friendly enough,' she added. 'We had coffee together in Wryton only yesterday.'

He looked surprised. Then, with a shrug of his shoulders, he patted the dog and called him on.

Maddy watched him walk away, fishing rod over his shoulder, and wondered what his problem was. She was still smarting as she retraced her steps back to the churchyard. She would speak to Tristan and get his permission and then she'd be able to thumb her nose at grumpy Ben Whatsisname.

* * *

Chloe Carson was waiting on the doorstep when she finally got back to the vicarage.

'I've had some ideas for the service,' the teenager said eagerly.

'Okay, you'd better come in.' Maddy turned the key in the lock. She felt concerned, for Chloe always seemed to be around. Didn't she have any friends of her own to hang out with? 'How did you get here today?' she asked worriedly.

'I got off the school bus at the top of the lane,' came the answer, followed by a, 'Wow! Look at all these books,' as Maddy led her into the small study.

'I'll go and make us some tea.'

When she returned with a tray she found Chloe running her hands over the book spines.

'I like this room,' Chloe said.

It looked out over the garden and a view of the lake.

'I'd put my desk by the window too if it was mine,' the teenager nodded her approval.

'Come on,' Maddy encouraged, sitting down in front of the computer. 'Give me your ideas; let's see what we can make of them.'

They spent an hour working together, drinking tea and nibbling chocolate biscuits. Every now and again Chloe's contributions would be interspersed with personal comments.

'Have you always wanted to be a vicar? Did you ever think of getting married? Is it alright living on your own? Because you know if you get lonely you could take in a lodger.'

'How are things at home?' Maddy questioned that last comment.

Sitting in the chair beside her Chloe turned and looked dreamily out of the window.

'They're alright,' she said distantly. 'Like, it's quiet now because the season's over.'

'What about friends? Do you have many friends?'

'Sometimes it's easier to be on your own,' Chloe turned to her, smiling sadly. 'You seem to manage it.'

'Oh Chloe,' Maddy shook her head. 'I'm so busy with people all day, I'm not really on my own.'

'Perhaps I'll be a vicar,' Chloe glanced at the books again.

Maddy took that opportunity to look briefly at her watch. It was almost seven.

'Right, that's enough work for this evening,' she said breezily. 'There's some good stuff here Chloe. I'll drive you home.'

Chloe retrieved her schoolbag from the hall.

'Do you know what?' Maddy said casually as she dropped her off at the gates to the boat yard. 'Next time you want to call give me a ring. It would be a pity if I wasn't there.'

In truth she didn't want her life taken over by unannounced visits, sensing that Chloe would be there all the time if she thought she could.

'Okay,' Chloe looked far from convinced.

'I'll see you in church on Sunday,' Maddy made the point gently, waving as she watched the fourteen year old go through the gates and disappear into the dark.

★　★　★

There was another church council meeting a few days later; Cecil Pugh had tabled a motion that they discuss finance, and much as Maddy wanted to sidestep the issue she knew it was unavoidable. There was a buzz of agitation as she entered the church hall.

'Cecil's up to something,' Ros warned. 'He's told a few people — his cronies — but there's definitely something going on.'

Maddy had always hated discussing money and buildings. She knew it was part of being a vicar but it was the most boring aspect of the job, a necessary evil. She preferred talking about people and missions and how to make things grow.

When they came to the finance item on the agenda Cecil Pugh took the floor, pedantically listing all the practical jobs that needed to be done. And, being a surveyor, he knew what he was talking about.

'It's all going to cost money — tens of thousands,' he pronounced and Maddy thought she detected relish in his tone. 'We have to do it to preserve these historic churches.'

Can't we close a couple of them and hand them over to Cadw? she thought subversively.

'But there's a more immediate cause

for concern,' he continued. 'As you know, the quarterly quota payment to the diocese is due. Yesterday I received this letter,' he found it in his file and held it up. 'It's from the solicitors for the Collet-Evans family informing us that as from today they are suspending all contributions to parish funds.'

A chorus of protest erupted. Smugly Cecil Pugh waved them to silence. Maddy was certain she'd had a letter from the solicitors too — it's just that she hadn't got around to opening it yet.

'Perhaps they don't like the way things are going,' he looked pointedly at Maddy.

She didn't know what to say in response.

'Be that as it may,' he surveyed them all rather grandly again. 'Our quota will be seriously short this quarter and without largesse from the estate I do not see how we could possibly be able to accomplish even a small percentage of the necessary works on all of our buildings.'

People came up with various suggestions, but the final concensus being that perhaps someone ought to try to persuade the family to change their minds.

'Well I could pay a call — I was very close with William as you all know,' Cecil puffed out his chest. A few people rolled their eyes.

'No, I'll go,' Maddy spoke up. 'I've called once already and I've had coffee at The Duke with Mr Collett-Evans.' Cecil Pugh shot her a surprised glance. He looked discomfited. 'And as vicar it really is my responsibility. I'm not doing the hard sell though,' she warned. 'Money isn't everything.' And after that she brought the meeting to a swift close.

★ ★ ★

It was something to be done sooner rather than later so the following day Maddy paid a visit to Collett Hall, taking the car this time as the rain was lashing down. Even the lake was obscured by a low lying mist. Tristan's car was on the drive. She didn't know whether to feel relieved that he was there or not.

In her hand she clutched the solicitor's letter she had now opened as Rita Teague showed her into the sitting room.

'I'll fetch Mr Collett-Evans for you, Vicar,' she said. 'I believe he's currently in the study.'

But only a few moments after she'd left Tristan appeared. Gone was the suit; he was wearing sweats, as if he'd just come from working out.

'Well hello,' he purred. 'Another visit from the vicar so soon. Are you trying to convert me?'

'I thought your family were church-goers,' she countered boldly.

'Well some of us more than others,' he grinned and spread himself out in a chair before the crackling fire. 'You're likely to be more persuasive than Malcolm though. I sat through some of his sermons as a child — God that man was boring!'

'You should come and hear mine,' said Maddy, flicking away the distaste she felt that he could be so dismissive of such a godly and hard working man.

'Perhaps I will, on Sunday.'

The elaborate clock on the mantelpiece chimed the hour, the fire spat in the grate and rain pitted the latticed windows. It was so relaxing in this room she almost felt like setting aside the reason for her visit and coming back another day. But she couldn't.

'Mr Collett-Evans,' she grasped the letter.

'Good God, call me Tristan! It's not like it's the first time we've met.'

'Tristan,' Maddy said with a smile. 'We had a church council meeting last night and we discussed the letter from your solicitors.'

'What letter?' he frowned.

'The one that says you're withdrawing all financial contributions to the parish. It's your prerogative of course, and I wouldn't want to pressure you, but in view of your family's connections with the church and the fact that we are four very small congregations which find it increasingly difficult to maintain the buildings and . . .'

'Ha!' he suddenly laughed cynically, startling her. Now it was Maddy's turn to frown. 'I know nothing about this, Vicar. It's nothing to do with me.'

'Oh,' Maddy was momentarily thrown, until she remembered that Cecil Pugh had mentioned a William, and suddenly she understood. 'Your father then . . .'

'My father's in a nursing home, completely cuckoo,' he wound a forefinger at his temple. 'But I know who the guilty party is and — well, well, right on time!'

Maddy followed his gaze to the door to see Ben coming into the room with the labrador trotting at his heels.

'Vicar, meet my older brother, Ben,' said Tristan. Then he tutted and shook his head. 'What have you been up to now, brother dear?'

5

It was not often that Maddy was lost for words. She sat open mouthed, trying to reconcile her assumption that he was the gardener with his true identity, wondering if she'd ever let slip to him her mistake, while Ben Collett-Evans stared silently back.

It was Tristan who broke the awkward moment.

'Ben's finally acquired power of attorney over our father's affairs,' he smiled mirthlessly at Maddy, 'and has wasted no time in flexing his muscles as lord of the manor.' He wagged his finger at him. 'Taking money from the church — that'll never get you to heaven, you know.'

For a moment Ben Collett-Evans looked incredibly angry, as if he actually wanted to strike out at his brother. The dog at his side glanced up at him fretfully for a few moments. Then he took a long, deep breath.

'There are more important things that need to be taken care of,' he said calmly. 'I'm sorry, Vicar,' he flicked hazel eyes at her, so different from his brother's. 'These are not easy times.'

'No they're not,' Maddy suddenly remembered Chloe. 'I was speaking with Lucas Carson the boat hire man the other day. He may have to go out of business because you're putting up the ground rent.'

'My father has not been well the past couple of years and matters have been . . . ' he paused and Maddy noticed the looks exchanged between brothers, ' . . . neglected. I'm simply trying to do what's best for the estate and our livelihood. Rents have to go up I'm afraid.'

'You know he's struggling to survive?' Maddy persisted. 'And raising a daughter alone. They live in a caravan.'

'As I say, I'm sorry.'

Maddy rose abruptly from her chair.

'Look, I'm only here about the church because my treasurer wanted me to come, but as far as I'm concerned if we can't repair the roof, we can't. And so what if the buildings fall down! It's people that matter. And Lucas Carson and his daughter matter. She's fourteen, do you know what a difficult age that is? She hasn't got a mother to talk to. Do you want to take her home away from her too?'

She appeared to have flummoxed him. She was aware of Tristan still seated, with a grin of admiration on his face. She waited for Ben Collett-Evans to come back at her. Instead he bent to scratch the labrador's ears and said, 'I'm not prepared to discuss it. Excuse me,' and left her and Tristan alone.

'Well!' Maddy, spoiling for a fight, felt angry that she'd been deprived of it. Short of following him from the room and haranguing him through the hallway of his own home there was nothing she could do.

'You're very impressive when you're angry, Vicar,' Tristan said at her shoulder. She looked into his amused blue eyes. 'It makes me want to ask you out.'

'Oh!'

'In fact, why don't I? The Duke has got a superb chef. When are you free?' Seeing she was perplexed, he laughed out loud. 'Am I allowed to ask a vicar out on a date?'

'Um, yes, of course,' Maddy blocked out the little voice in her head that was telling her to remember Michael and did she really want to go there again? You can't trust any of them! She searched for her diary in her bag. 'Friday's free,' she said.

'Friday it is then,' Tristan declared, sounding pleased with himself. 'And Vicar, don't worry. I'll have a word with Ben, see what I can do to ease his draconian measures.'

'Thank you. I'd be very grateful.'

★　★　★

'I'm sorry but I can't make Ben change his mind about the money,' Tristan said, handing back the menus after they'd ordered their starters. The restaurant was busy and there were some very enticing smells emanating from the kitchen.

'Well you tried,' Maddy assured him. She tasted the wine — it was surprisingly good. All around them well-heeled diners engaged in conversation to the accompaniment of a man in a bow tie playing a piano near the french windows opening out onto a fairylit courtyard.

This evening she'd worn a black jersey dress and now she found herself wondering if the neckline was too low — Tristan's gaze seemed to be drawn to it frequently. She was so unused to dressing up to go out these days. The usual tied-back blonde hair was blow dried so that it tumbled about her shoulders. Did it make her look like a wanton? She was a single thirty-two-year-old woman though. She cleared her throat and tried not to focus on herself.

'I have a feeling you and your brother don't get on,' she said.

'I've never liked his holier than thou attitude,' Tristan replied. 'I've tried to make something of myself apart from the estate, moving out to London. He's got a thing against me, I don't know what.' Tristan shrugged. 'Of course, now he's finally managed to get power of attorney over our father's affairs . . . '

'How long has your father been ill?'

'It started about four years ago. He began to get forgetful, couldn't do certain things. Once we got a diagnosis of Alzheimer's he rapidly went downhill.'

'What about your mother?'

'Died in a car crash abroad when I was fifteen.'

'I'm so sorry, that must have been awful. So is it just you and your brother now?'

'We had a sister, Rebecca. She died three years ago. Yes, tragic isn't it?' he smiled cynically. 'Just because we're an old, supposedly wealthy family, people think we're lucky.' He took a sip of his wine. 'You've heard about the curse no doubt?'

Maddy nodded. 'I think it's a load of rubbish, superstitious nonsense. Obviously, I don't believe in things like that,' she replied.

'Nor do I. Stories for old women to gossip over. Ah, here we are . . . '

The first course was served and for a while they ate in silence.

'May I ask why you're still single?' Tristan said presently.

'There was someone in my last parish,' Maddy said, feeling very guarded about sharing something personal which still hurt. 'But I'm afraid it didn't work out.'

'If he left you he must have been mad!'

Maddy looked away from his blue eyes and picked up her glass, looking around the restaurant. Tristan was very good at making her feel appreciated, almost as if he had a natural knack for it which made her feel naturally wary.

But as the evening wore on the good food, wine, music and the warmth of the fire crackling in the large stone grate made her feel relaxed and replete. At the end of the night, like a true gentleman, he helped her into her coat squeezing her shoulders, his lips tantalisingly close to her ear.

Climbing into his expensive car gave her a buzz even though she knew she shouldn't be impressed by material things. As they roared along the dark country lanes, listening to some jazz on the radio, Maddy wondered if she were going to go out with him again if he asked her, trying not to let her imagination gallop too far ahead.

When he finally pulled up at the bottom of the lane under the one street lamp that served both church and vicarage he told her to wait there. He got out and hurried around to open the door for her.

'Thank you,' she said as he helped her out of the low-slung seat.

'I had a good time. Shall I come in?'

'No, I'm the vicar!'

As if anyone was going to see them out here in the middle of nowhere. Obviously thinking the same thing, he chuckled.

'I'll walk you to the door, then.'

'No, I'll be fine,' Maddy assured him. 'I'll —'

Before she could say anything else he leaned into her and kissed her, a very knowledgeable kiss that set her senses reeling.

'Couldn't help myself,' he grinned when they drew apart. 'Never kissed a vicar before.'

'I'm certainly glad you didn't try it with Malcolm!' Maddy quipped. She felt disorientated. It was all going too fast, it was a little bit too easy.

Tristan said goodnight before getting back into the car and roaring off into the night. Humming to herself Maddy fumbled for her keys in her bag. As she reached the porch she jumped as something or someone moved quickly and came into the pool of the bright security light.

68

'Chloe!' she sighed, relieved it wasn't an intruder. 'What are you doing here at this time of night?'

'I wanted to talk.'

'But it's ... ' she looked at her watch, ' ... ten thirty. Does your dad know you're here?'

'I saw you kissing him,' Chloe said and Maddy knew she wasn't referring to her father. 'Do you love him?'

'What? No! I barely know him. We've just been for a meal.'

'You shouldn't have gone with him. He's a Collett-Evans. Don't you know what he's doing to us!'

'Yes, and Tristan's tried to talk to his brother.'

'They're evil! All of them!'

'Chloe, nobody's evil,' Maddy sighed. 'Except maybe Hitler and ... let's not have a debate about it now. You'd better come in.'

Maddy put the key in the lock and led her inside, all the warm loved-up feelings of the evening quickly dissipating in the light of the teenager's attitude.

'Can I stay with you tonight?' Chloe begged. It was then Maddy noticed her red rimmed eyes, as if she'd been crying.

'Is everything alright at home?' she asked concerned.

'It's Dylan, in school,' her lip quivered. 'I thought he liked me, but he was just using me. I'll never have a boyfriend!'

Maddy made her a hot drink, leaving her in the kitchen while she rang Lucas Carson. He was relieved to find out where his daughter had disappeared to and gave his consent for her to stay. Maddy made up a bed in one of the guest rooms, turning on the radiator to get rid of the damp chill. Then she listened to Chloe pouring out her woes.

'He said he was my boyfriend,' she screwed up her face. 'He even kissed me once, and he was always writing me notes. Then I found out that Jessica Rees and Sarah Bolt had put him up to it for a bet.'

Maddy put a comforting arm around her.

'Nobody'll ever love me. I'll never have a boyfriend!'

'Yes you will,' Maddy assured. 'It's just that when you're fourteen things seem complicated. But you've got years and years to meet someone.'

'I can't talk to my dad.'

'Well dads are a bit different from mums.'

'You look nice tonight,' Chloe suddenly sat up, wiping her nose and her tears with the back of her hand.

'Thank you,' Maddy said. She was suddenly intensely aware that she smelt of garlic and woodsmoke — and of Tristan's aftershave.

'It's a pity that it had to be him though.'

'Right, time for bed!' Maddy said decisively, unwilling to discuss Tristan any further. 'Things will look better in the morning.'

Afterwards she sat alone at the kitchen table, cradling a coffee mug in her hands, mulling over the evening's events. She could see her reflection against the black of the night through the kitchen window. Who was the woman staring back? Sometimes her identity was so tied up with being a vicar she didn't know how to be anyone else. Tristan had made her feel special tonight, but he was a smooth operator. Too smooth? She cast aside her niggles and allowed herself to bask in the warmth of the romantic evening.

Then she thought of Chloe. It was plain that she couldn't be a mother substitute to her — it wasn't professional. In the morning she would have to figure out what to do.

With a sigh she tipped away the dregs of her coffee in the sink, turned off the light and went to bed.

6

In the morning Chloe wanted to join her in church for morning prayer. They were both coming out of the vicarage when Maddy saw Cecil Pugh returning to his car. He stopped to regard them both together with an element of surprise.

'Good morning, Vicar,' he sniffed. 'I've just been into church to check the collection entry in the service book for last Sunday.'

'We're heading there now,' Maddy swallowed her dislike of the man. 'Would you care to join us?'

'No time, sorry,' he said quickly before opening the door of his car and getting in.

'I don't like him,' Chloe observed as he drove away. 'He's mean.'

Good observation, Maddy wanted to say but didn't of course.

'What are you going to do today?' Maddy asked after they'd said their prayers together.

Chloe shrugged in reply.

'I've got visiting to get on with, and I need to prepare for tomorrow,' Maddy said firmly, 'So I'll take you home first.'

After she'd dropped off the teenager Maddy called in on Ros who was in her pottery shed.

'The boys are out working on the farm with Tim,' Ros explained their absence. 'It's a busy time on a farm so I won't see them all day.'

Maddy told her about Chloe's overnight stay and her growing concern about the teenager.

'She needs a mother figure,' she concluded, 'and I can't be that.'

'She is a little intense,' Ros mused. 'A bit too pre-occupied with religion and obsessed with that stupid legend, but a good kid for all that. I tell you what,' she examined the pot she'd finished painting, 'bring her over here next time. Maybe I can help. But enough of

Chloe, you said you were coming back from dinner with Tristan Collett-Evans.'

Maddy told her the details.

'It was a great night,' she played with a clay knife on the bench.

'Are you going to go if he asks you out again?'

'I think I'll see if he turns up in church tomorrow. He keeps threatening to.'

Ros chuckled. 'That'll be the day.'

'That sounds ominous.'

'It's just that we haven't seen much of him around here,' her new found friend explained.

Maddy tapped the knife against the edge of the bench.

'I'll wait and see,' she said.

★ ★ ★

Tristan wasn't in church the following morning. Cecil Pugh was though and wasted no time in coming up to her in the vestry afterwards and asking her if she'd been up to Collett Hall. Maddy

75

stepped back from his jabbing finger.

'Yes,' she said. 'They're not going to change their minds.'

At that he stormed off mumbling that it was a man's job and he'd better do it himself. Then Klara Robinson put her head around the door.

'Vicar, I've come to tell you that I'm not happy with the direction the music is going. I'm resigning as organist.'

'Oh, Klara, don't do that!'

But the woman shook her head and left.

'A lot of people are finding this transition difficult,' Ken warned. 'And now the loss of the Collett-Evans' money has hit them hard.'

'People need to learn that we pay our own way,' Maddy said defiantly. 'The days of relying on handouts have gone!'

But for all her bravado she felt beleaguered by her worried congregations for the rest of the day — and disappointed that Tristan had not turned up.

She paid Klara Robinson a visit the following morning. She lived in a pretty cottage on the other side of the lake with lace curtains at the windows, floral bone china on display and rose patterned cushions on her squashy sofa. Try as she might Maddy could not persuade her to change her mind.

'If you want modern music then that's what you'll have to settle for every week. I'm not happy, Vicar. I've been going to Saint David's for forty years. Malcolm would never have done this!'

No, but I'm not Malcolm, Maddy wanted to say. She left the now ex-organist, disappointed that things had not worked out.

One of the messages on her answering machine when she got back was from Tristan.

'Apologies for Sunday,' he said brightly, sounding as if he wasn't sorry at all. 'Got some good news for you. Call me.'

Good news — she could do with

some of that. With heart racing she dialled his number. He answered almost immediately.

'Ah, gave you up for lost,' he said.

'I work other days apart from Sundays,' she reminded him.

'Really?' he teased. 'Well stop working now and come up to the house as soon as you can.'

He didn't say why and she didn't ask. Putting on her coat again she went out and within five minutes was ringing the doorbell at Collett Hall.

Tristan was in the sitting room, flicking through papers on the coffee table. At his side was a cafetière and two cups. Seeing her he got up from his chair with a grin.

'Ah, the prompt vicar,' he kissed her on the cheek. 'Coffee?'

She sat on the sofa opposite him and watched him pour. His sleeves were rolled up revealing tanned arms.

Stop it! she chided herself, still thinking about the kiss.

'What is it?' he seemed to pick up on

it as he leant across and handed her a cup.

'Nothing. What's the good news?'

'Ah, I've persuaded Ben to let you walk over our land whenever you feel you want to.'

'Oh.'

'You look disappointed.'

'No, it's great!' She'd rather been expecting something more along the lines of he's not raising Lucas Carson's rent and he's re-instating the Collett-Evans' badly needed regular contribution to the church funds.

He laughed. 'There is more actually. I'm expecting a profit on some of my investments. It won't be much but I'll do what I can,' he shrugged.

'I'd rather have you in church than your money,' Maddy said boldly.

'Come on!' he said, suddenly getting up from his chair. 'I'll give you a tour of the house.'

Forgetting her coffee Maddy followed him around, marvelling as they went from room to room, all of them

79

grand and each filled with fine paintings and antiques.

'You could get lost in a house like this,' she whispered.

'We had great games of hide and seek when we were small.'

'And the paintings,' Maddy looked up as they ended up back in the hall. 'Are they all your ancestors?'

'Yup. Those are my parents.' He was standing right behind her, his mouth close to her ear as he pointed out a canvas in oils at the bottom of the stairs. He was too close for propriety, but Maddy didn't mind, feeling a frisson of excitement.

'I can see the likeness,' she said.

William Collett-Evans was very handsome with dark hair and brooding eyes. Tristan had inherited his mother's blue eyes and lazy mouth, a combination which made the woman in the painting look slightly haughty.

She was about to say something profound when a mobile phone rang. Tristan stepped away, fishing a tiny handset out of his pocket, and began to speak. As he did so she realised that Ben had appeared in the hallway and had witnessed the intimate moment and her appraisal of the painting. She observed that he looked more like his father. He watched them now with some of that brooding intensity.

'Sorry, Vicar, I've got to go,' Tristan snapped the handset shut again, then, seeing his brother, added wickedly. 'Feel free to walk over our land anytime you want to.'

Then he was gone and Maddy was left wondering awkwardly what to do. Ben Collett-Evans continued to regard her for a moment before saying something which set her on edge and annoyed her because it spoiled what had been a lovely half hour, 'Don't take my brother at face value Miss Green. He likes to make promises and win friends.'

'Well at least one of you does!' she said tartly. 'Good day.'

7

Maddy had roped Ros into helping prepare the youth service. So far Chloe had managed to persuade a couple of girls from school to come along and Ros' boys were there along with some of the slightly younger children.

'We'll do something spectacular for Christmas,' Chloe had said. 'A super nativity with bells and whistles.'

Maddy dreaded to think what that would involve but she was just glad to see Chloe excited about something. She and Ros sat in one of the pews and watched now.

'Have you seen Tristan again?' Ros asked.

Maddy shook her head. 'Not since that day he disappeared so quickly. Not a peep.' She had wondered about it before dismissing it. It wasn't as if they were going out after all — she'd only had one meal with him. 'He just seems so affable and interested and then,' she made a gesture with her hand. 'Anyway,' she wanted to change the subject. 'How are you getting on with Chloe?'

'Strange kid, hard to get close to,' Ros frowned. 'You're the one she's taken a shine to. When I asked her around the other day she kept banging on about the curse — you know, Letty Pendle and all that. She's convinced that something bad is going to happen. In the end I had to ask her to stop because she was worrying the boys. She wouldn't open up about anything personal.'

'Give it time,' Maddy said, watching the teenager organising her little group. Sensing she was being watched Chloe suddenly turned around and gave her a bright yet brittle smile. Chloe had turned up on her doorstep twice more late at night and although Maddy had been firm on one occasion, driving her home, the teenager had been so distraught on the other that she had allowed her to stay. She wondered what she was going to do with her.

★ ★ ★

The letter was buried underneath the rest of the post and looked fairly insignificant — a white, cheap envelope. When she opened it the first thing Maddy noticed was that it was stamped with the address of the bishop's office. Expecting it to be one of the regular circulars she was shocked to discover its contents — an invitation to meet with Bishop Wyn at ten thirty on Wednesday to discuss some of the concerns about the parish. What concerns? She'd certainly divulged none. She didn't have any concerns! Then Maddy gave a cynical smile. Cecil Pugh had obviously been busy.

On Wednesday she presented herself at the bishop's palace in Wryton, a seventeenth century timber and brick building next to the cathedral with extensive rose gardens still in bloom in November.

She didn't really know Bishop Wyn having only met him once at her induction. Alice, his secretary, showed her into a spotless study.

'Ah Madeleine,' he rose from his chair behind a desk on which stood a streamlined laptop and a couple of books. 'Come in, sit down. Would you make some tea, Alice?'

Maddy sat down. She knew the bishop was a family man in his late fifties, fastidious in his style — after all he'd once been a high flying London lawyer — his churchmanship just the right side of accepting women as priests.

'How are things going in the parish?' he invited.

Her previous bishop, Bill, had been a true pastor. She felt that Bishop Wyn wanted to dissect her.

'Fine. I've started up some new things, tried to get more young people involved.'

'Young people involvement. Yes, that's

always a good thing, although I find it's a fine line between welcoming the new and yet not alienating the old.'

Before Maddy could comment the secretary returned with the tea.

'Thank you, Alice,' said the bishop pleasantly. He served them both then sat back in his chair. 'Where were we?'

'The old and the new.'

'Yes. I'll come straight to the point Madeleine. Some people have been expressing concern.'

'Who?'

'You know I can't reveal names. Suffice to say I've had some letters. I am here to support you, of course, you are the vicar and it is up to you what you do in the parish. Those who object to women clerics on principle will just have to get used to it.'

Maddy held the cup and saucer in her hands. She hadn't touched the tea, far more focussed on preparing to defend herself.

'There is another concern,' Bishop Wyn laid a hand on a sheet of paper on his desk, the morning light catching the ring on his finger. 'This quarter's quota is well short for the first time in years. Why do you think the parish is having difficulty in paying?'

Maddy explained about the Collett-Evans' contribution. He appeared to consider that for a brief moment before saying, 'The parish must be able to pay its way.'

'We will.'

Bishop Wyn sipped his tea. 'There is one other thing,' he said, replacing the cup on the saucer carefully. 'How many years have you been in ministry?'

'Seven.'

'Then you know our behaviour must be above board. There must be no reason for people to criticise us.'

Maddy frowned, wondering where this was leading.

'In the light of child protection and everything that surrounds it, it may not, as in the past, be appropriate for you to be alone overnight with a teenage parishioner.'

Maddy sat back in her seat, stunned.

'The girl was seen coming out of the vicarage one morning. Now while I am sure it was an act of pastoral care on your part, in these litigous times others might misconstrue.'

Cecil Pugh! He had been coming out of church that morning and seen them together. How could he! Maddy was lost for words.

'I am sure you are a conscientious priest in charge,' Bishop Wyn smiled. 'Please consider what I've said.'

The meeting was over. Maddy felt dazed as she came away, betrayed by Cecil and others, furious that she couldn't even offer a bed for the night to a child in distress. And why had Bishop Wyn pointedly addressed her as priest in charge? Because as such — unlike being an incumbent of a parish and possessor of the freehold — she could be dismissed if the bishop saw good reason.

Shock gave way to anger as she drove out of the cathedral grounds. Suddenly the last thing she wanted to do was go back to the parish. Instead she turned down the hill and into the town, leaving the car in the supermarket car park.

Maddy walked down the High Street, head down, hands tucked into her coat pockets. She went into the quirky Country Store for a little retail therapy searching through the racks of distinctive clothing, finally realising that buying things was not the answer.

She looked at the sales assistant and for a moment wished they could swap places. Why couldn't she have a nine-to-five job that demanded little and meant she could switch off when she got home?

Gradually Maddy calmed down and because she felt guilty for spending so much time browsing she purchased a couple of scented candles, tucked them away in her bag, and stepped out into the street once more. It was market day and the town was buzzing. She looked at the clock over the town hall — too early to go back, not while she was still seething inside.

The Duke beckoned a welcome. Maddy crossed the busy road and went into the coffee shop next to the restaurant, ordering a strong black coffee and the gooiest cake they had on the trolley.

For a while she watched the world go by outside the window. Just at the very moment she turned away she saw a familiar figure through the glass doors between the coffee shop and the restaurant — Tristan.

Maddy called for the bill and left payment plus a tip on the plate. She could do with cheering up. Perhaps he'd share another coffee with her. She paused on the threshold to the restaurant as she realised Tristan was not alone. There was a woman with perfectly straight blonde hair and a made-up face that screamed money and know how. Maddy watched him pull out a chair for her.

'I've missed you darling,' the woman

said as Tristan sat opposite. She reached out a hand and traced the line of his cheek and jaw. 'What's been happening while I've been away?'

'Absolutely nothing,' he answered. 'Which is why I'm glad you're back. Liven up this dull place a bit.'

Maddy almost gagged as he leant across the table and kissed her, not a peck on the cheek, but a full-blown intimate kiss.

'Excuse me madam,' a waiter said as she almost careered into him in her haste to escape. She said a quick apology and ran out of The Duke into the street.

The phone rang as she was storming down the High Street and Maddy fumbled for it in her bag. It was Ros, just the person she needed to speak to to get things off her chest. But before she could say anything Ros spoke first in a voice which didn't sound like hers — rushed and breathless.

'Maddy, can you come? There's been an accident. It's Ethan, he's badly hurt.

I'm at the hospital in the city. I don't know if . . . ' Ros choked.

'I'm setting off now,' Maddy assured her, all thoughts of Tristan and the bishop forgotten.

It was a thirty five mile drive along country lanes to the city and by the time Maddy had found the hospital the afternoon was closing in with a light drizzle falling. It suited her mood as she searched for a parking space then looked around for the main entrance to the building. When she reached A & E and enquired after Ethan Lannigan she was told he'd gone into surgery and would be returning to the children's ward.

Finally she found Ros sitting alone in a waiting room, an undrunk plastic cup of coffee on the table at her side. Her friend bounded out of her chair as soon as she saw Maddy.

'I came as soon as I got your message,' Maddy hugged her. 'What's happened?'

'Ethan was out with Tim on the

tractor up at Maes Goch,' Ros said, returning to her seat. 'Tim swears he doesn't know how it happened but Ethan fell out. He was lucky the tractor didn't crush him.'

'How is he?' Maddy sat next to her friend.

'He took a knock on the head but they think that will be alright,' Ros looked distracted, her fingers playing along her thigh. 'He's broken his leg and cracked a couple of ribs too. He's in theatre now.'

'Poor lamb,' Maddy commisserated. 'Where's Tim?'

'Someone had to stay at home with Josh.'

'You should have called me! I would have had him.'

'To be honest we weren't thinking straight,' Ros gave a watery smile.

'Well I'm here now.'

They sat waiting for what seemed like hours, sometimes chatting, sometimes not. Ros suddenly jumped out of her chair as a bed was wheeled past the open door. A nurse stopped her.

'Give us five minutes to settle him Mrs Lannigan,' she said kindly. 'The operation went well.'

Ros couldn't sit still, pacing the floor like a caged animal. She almost shoved the nurse out of the way when she came to say they could go in.

Maddy followed at a more sedate pace. When she got to the bed Ros was leaning over her son brushing back the hair from his forehead, clasping his hand and muttering comforting words. 'It's alright, Mummy's here.'

Maddy could see that he hadn't fully come round from the anaesthetic as he whimpered pathetically. Poor kid, he'd be feeling sorry for himself for a while.

'Ros!'

Maddy turned to see Tim hurrying down the ward.

'Where's Josh?' Ros responded.

'Bill and Ava have taken him. How is he?'

Maddy watched as they fussed over their child.

'Listen,' she said, 'I'll leave you two alone for a while. I'll come back in half an hour.'

She didn't know what she was going to do. No one from the parish was in hospital. There was always the restaurant though — if she could find it in this maze of a place!

Turning the corner she found herself in another corridor. Overhead signs pointed to ICU. She stopped as ahead she saw a familiar figure walking away — Ben Collett-Evans — and felt relieved he was going in the opposite direction and hadn't seen her; she didn't really fancy another confrontation.

Why was he here? She mused, until she remembered that his father had dementia. Maybe he'd been taken seriously ill. She traced the squares on the lino with the toe of her shoe as she considered what to do next. He was Tristan's father too and Tristan had shown no antipathy towards her. Perhaps she could offer some spiritual help.

One of the good things about wearing a dog collar was that staff in hospitals didn't question her requests to see people.

'Hello,' she smiled, drawing up at the desk just outside the unit. 'I'm the Reverend Maddy Green from the Parish of Llwyn Ddu. Do you have a Mr Collett-Evans here?'

'Ben was just visiting,' the pleasant faced nurse replied. 'Do you mean Miss Collett-Evans?'

For a moment Maddy was flummoxed.

'Rebecca Collett-Evans,' the nurse prompted.

Rebecca! Rebecca was dead wasn't she? She was certain Tristan had told her he had a sister who'd died. She squashed down her confusion and smiled back.

'Yes, of course, Rebecca.'

The nurse pressed a buzzer on her desk.

'Go in please.'

Maddy pushed through the double

doors. Once inside they clicked shut again. The lighting was dim in here and she could hear machines beeping and whirring. Now, how was she going to find Rebecca Collett-Evans when she didn't have a clue what she looked like?

She stopped one of the male nurses dressed in blue coveralls.

'Hi, I'm looking for Rebecca Collett-Evans. I'm the parish priest but I'm new so I've never met her.'

'Did you see Ben?' said the man — Nurse Dyer according to the name tag. 'He just left a moment ago.'

'We must have missed each other.'

'Rebecca's is the last room on the right,' he pointed down a short corridor. 'She won't respond to you but we still talk to her and tell her exactly what we're doing.'

His bright, conversational manner was in sharp contrast to the seriousness of the unit. Maddy's heart was racing as she approached the last glass-fronted room. She was about to see a dead woman — or someone she'd believed to be dead. Why had Tristan lied to her?

The woman lay quite still on the bed, tubes in her nose and running into other parts of her body under the sheet. Her blonde hair was splayed out on the pillow. Her face, which Maddy could see had once been beautiful, was swollen, the eyes unseeing. The mouth looked too small to contain the protruding tongue. Maddy saw how her hands were curled over. She recognised all the symptoms of PVS.

Maddy let out a long sigh. Why keep this a secret? Why say she was dead? And how had she come to this? She moved forward and instinctively reached out to touch the bare arm.

'Hello Rebecca,' she said. 'I'm Maddy the new vicar. I know your brother Tristan, and I've met Ben too. I've just discovered by chance that you're here and I'm very pleased to meet you.'

'What the hell are you doing here?'

Maddy swung round to see Ben Collett-Evans in the doorway.

'Who gave you permission?' he looked livid.

'I'm sorry,' she stepped back from the bed. 'I saw you outside and assumed it was your father. I didn't know your sister was still alive; Tristan said she'd died.'

'You have no right to be here,' he came into the room inching her out of the way. 'What gives you the right to impose yourself on my family?'

'I beg your pardon.' Maddy spoke up for herself. 'I know your brother well for a start, I'm the parish priest and I'm just doing my duty.'

'We don't need your prayers, for all the good they do.'

Maddy was surprised at the level of vitriol.

'I want you to leave, please.'

'Of course I will if you don't want me here,' Maddy agreed, her acquiescence taking the wind out of his sails. 'It was a genuine mistake. I really did expect it to be your father.'

But he wasn't listening, all his

attention directed towards the unmoving figure in the bed. He looked quite loving and tender which was at odds with his abrasiveness towards her thus far.

'I will pray for your sister and your family,' she said, at the door. He didn't look up and she left him there.

'Oh, did you manage to catch Ben?' Nurse Dyer looked up with a smile. 'It's been three years but he still visits twice every single week.'

What a tragic family, Maddy felt sorry for them. Then she suddenly thought of what Chloe had said the other day. Maddy didn't believe in curses — a gypsy had once told her she would be dead before she was thirty and her faith had made a mockery of that — but three things in one day — the bishop, Tristan and now Ethan.

She shook herself and hurried back to her friend.

8

Maddy slept fitfully that night, her dreams full of Tristan kissing women and laughing at her, and Rebecca Collett-Evans rising grotesquely from her sick bed and chasing her through endless hospital corridors. When she awoke it was still dark, Daylight came only grudgingly this time of year and the sun took a while to struggle over the eastern hills. She lay in bed, ruminating over the previous day's events, trying to make some sense of them, and when she couldn't she decided to get up and go into church early to say morning prayer.

There was frost in the air so she pulled on an extra cardigan and a scarf and hat. Mist obscured the lake, creeping through the reeds and up the lane; the birds in the trees were silent. The church seemed to glower at her as she approached the door. When she tried to turn the key in the lock she discovered that the door was already open.

Well it couldn't be Cecil or Ken, not at seven thirty in the morning and besides which there was no car in the lane. She pulled back the heavy curtain which kept the draughts out to see Ben Collett-Evans standing in the aisle, seemingly reading the marble plaques on the walls.

He looked around as he heard the noise.

'I thought I'd be alone,' he said.

'You would have been. I don't normally come across so early to say morning prayer. How did you get in?'

'The family has a key.'

He continued to read the plaques. Maddy waited, not wanting to drive him out yet equally certain that she couldn't begin her prayers while he was here.

'All these people,' he finally said, 'all dead. They believed once. Do you suppose it made any difference?' he turned to give her a long and cynical look.

'Oh yes, I believe it does,' Maddy was careful not to sound too fervent. She advanced slowly down the aisle, arms clasped firmly about her against the cold.

'I sang in the choir and was a server in this church when I was a boy,' Ben said. 'Faith was simple until I grew up. How do you deal in the simple, Vicar?' he looked at her accusingly.

'If only it was,' she countered. 'I find faith infinitely complex. Sometimes I can't make any sense of it.'

'An honest vicar.'

Maddy felt she knew what he was referring to.

'I'm sorry about yesterday,' she said. 'I genuinely thought I was going to see your father.'

'And then you thought you could fix it did you?'

'No.'

'Some things can never be fixed.

103

Sometimes faith is not enough.'

'Then what are you doing here?'

He stared at her for a long moment, his gaze reminding her how different he was to Tristan, the eyes deep and unfathomable. It looked as if he hadn't even combed his hair after tumbling out of bed. Underneath his Barbour he wore a woollen jumper that had bobbled with age and frequent washing.

'Just curious,' he answered presently.

'It must be difficult, with your father and your sister, taking over the running of the estate . . . '

'You really have no idea, Miss Green.'

'Why don't you call me Maddy?'

'They can't do anymore for her you know,' he looked away to the east window where the sun had just reached the topmost part, golding the crown of Christ in glory and sending shafts of sunlight across old wooden pews and crumbling flagstones. 'I don't know why we don't finish it. After all there are no miracles, are there?'

Sensing it was a rhetorical question Maddy left it unanswered. He turned back and, shoving hands into his coat pockets said brusquely, 'I'll leave you to your prayers.'

'You could pray with me.'

'I'm afraid I'm not good enough.' The bleakness of his expression took Maddy's breath away. 'And if there is such a thing as divine forgiveness it's not for the likes of me.'

She watched him leave the church, the door crashing on its hinges behind him, before looking up at the golden window. Whatever had happened to give Ben Collett-Evans such a low opinion of himself? She was determined to get to the bottom of it.

★　★　★

'Hasn't anybody told you about it?' Ros was opening a bag of crisps for Ethan as he lay with his head turned towards the television.

Two days after the accident he was

beginning to recover from the trauma and there were glimmerings of him enjoying his position as the subject of so much attention.

'Well Tristan said he had a sister who had died . . . '

'How unbelievable! Probably ashamed. Old families have their secrets.'

'Mum,' Ethan whined and Ros handed him the crisps before sitting down again.

'So . . . ?' Maddy encouraged, intrigued.

'It happened down at the lake about three years ago. Rebecca had brought some friends down from university. They were messing about on the water and Rebecca fell in.' She lowered her voice. 'There was talk of them taking stuff they shouldn't have been. Apparently it took a while for them to pull her out. They gave her the kiss of life but she had injuries, too.'

Maddy frowned.

'Why would Ben Collett-Evans feel so personally responsible?' she asked. 'I really sensed yesterday that he was like a man with something on his conscience.'

Ros shook her head.

'I know what Chloe would say — it's the Letty Pendle curse.'

'There's something else too,' this time Maddy lowered her voice as she told her friend about seeing Tristan and the woman at The Duke.

'Were you really sweet on him?' Ros commiserated.

'Nah,' said Maddy but she knew that she was lying to herself.

★ ★ ★

Tristan rang to ask if she'd like to go up to the house for coffee.

'We didn't finish our tour last time.'

'I'm sorry, I'm busy today,' Maddy declined.

'Really? Can't you fit in an odd half hour? Come for lunch if you like.'

'Thanks but I can't.'

'Oh, okay then.' He sounded puzzled at the unexpected brush off.

107

Madddy tried to put him out of her mind; she'd been taken in, she'd fallen for him too quickly. Stupid! She found herself thinking of Ben a lot though, intrigued by their encounter in church and the mystery that seemed to surround him. Why come to church if he was so against faith? Was there still a vestige of something there?

On Sunday she was surprised to see Tristan sitting in the family pew. He watched her throughout the whole service, appreciative of her sermon, impressed by the way she did things; it was enough to turn a woman's head. And afterwards, when people had gone, he sidled up.

'See, I've finally had to come to you,' he smiled. 'If this was your plan then it's worked.'

'I don't do plans,' Maddy said churlishly. 'Unlike some people.'

'That's the faith bit I suppose,' he took her hand between his gloved hands. 'Shall we have lunch one day this week? I can book The Duke.'

'I'm too busy,' Maddy withdrew her hand.

'Vicar, you're making me chase you,' he chided with a twinkle in his eye. 'But that's okay, I like the chase.'

He sounded so confident of catching her! Maddy felt affronted. She could have said *Who did I see you with in The Duke the other day?* but wasn't going to justify her rejection of him. And why had he lied about his sister? There were obviously other things he could lie about too.

'Well if you want to continue the pursuit I'm here next Sunday,' she said dismissively.

He looked at her curiously as if he couldn't work out why she appeared to have changed. Then Miriam Lovelace was butting in, hand extended as she gushed over him, declaring how wonderful it was to see a member of the family in church once more. Maddy ducked away into the vestry to disrobe where Cecil Pugh's superior face greeted her.

'I heard you had a meeting with the bishop,' he said as he emptied the collection into a bag for banking.

'Yes I did,' said Maddy, adding in a tone which invited no discussion, 'And it was very fruitful.'

Ken Williams exchanged a glance with her.

'Don't worry about it,' he whispered after Cecil had gone. 'He's a stirrer. The majority of us are behind you.'

'Thanks Ken.' That made her feel warm inside.

Chloe was hanging around at the back of the church waiting for her.

'I've got to go to Saint Non's for the eleven o'clock,' Maddy reminded her.

'Yes, I know. I was actually wondering if maybe I could come around this week, you know, to talk about the service,' she said shyly.

'I thought you were going to get the group together for that.'

'I thought I could stay with you overnight,' Chloe traced a loose pattern on the stack of prayer books.

'Listen Chloe,' Maddy sighed. 'You can't. I mean, I can't have you in the vicarage overnight.'

'Oh,' her face fell.

'It's not deemed appropriate these days. It's because I'm on my own. I have to cover myself.'

Chloe looked at her for a moment, mouth turned down, then she turned on her heel and fled from the church.

★ ★ ★

Ethan came home from hospital a few days later. Maddy told Ros about Chloe.

'Well now I'm home let's see if I can make another attempt with her and take the burden off you,' Ros said helpfully.

'I think I've really upset her,' Maddy shook her head. 'She hasn't called at the vicarage since.'

So concerned was Maddy that she drove over to see Lucas Carson. He opened the door to the caravan almost

111

as soon as she knocked and invited her in. The table was strewn with invoices, bills and a calculator.

'Just trying to balance the books,' he said with a thin smile.

It made her angry to think of Ben Collett-Evans with all his money and the big house putting up the rent on a small business and probably forcing it to the wall.

Lucas Carson offered her some refreshments but she declined coming straight to the point and telling him about how and why she'd had to refuse having Chloe to stay overnight.

'I want to be a friend to her but I have to be careful.'

'Of course, Vicar. I'm pleased she's got an interest in the church. It might help her get through the difficult times ahead.'

Maddy glanced at the papers spread out across the table.

'Is it that bad?'

Lucas Carson sighed. 'With the rent going up so much I think we'll have to move on. I don't know where to or even if I'll be able to get a job. We won't have a home; this caravan is part of the property.'

'Something will turn up,' Maddy reassured him, not feeling particularly confident that it would. One thing was clear: she had to try to persuade Ben Collett-Evans to change his mind.

9

It was a cold, crisp morning, a foretaste of the coming winter. Advent Sunday was on the horizon. Maddy walked up to Collett Hall. The cars were in the drive. When she arrived at the main entrance she found the door ajar. She knocked first and when nobody came to answer she stepped inside, closing the door behind her.

'Hello?' she called out.

There was no response. Yet somebody was obviously home. Maddy crossed to the sitting room where she'd had her previous meetings with Tristan. There was a fire crackling in the grate but the room was empty. None of the other rooms leading off the main hallway yielded satisfaction so Maddy set off into the east wing, recalling from that day Tristan had given her a tour of the house that the study was located in that part of the big house.

At last she heard voices; they were raised in a heated discussion. She recognised them as belonging to Ben and Tristan.

She paused on the threshold to the study; through the half-open door she could see Ben seated at the desk and his brother standing over him, gesticulating angrily.

'Why should I listen to you? If father hadn't gone cuckoo you wouldn't be in this position!' Tristan was saying.

'It's because he was getting ill you were able to take advantage,' came the reply. 'If I hadn't done something, Tris, you would have eventually bled us dry.'

'My investments are about to pay off!'

'In this economic climate?'

'I just need more money — and you've cut me off.'

'Your investments have never made money. Whatever money father gave you you've wasted on your wild ideas and your women and the estate has paid for it. I'm trying to hold it all together,' Ben caught up a sheaf of papers from the desk, 'and you're fighting me every step of the way because you resent me being the eldest.'

Maddy could see Tristan's face twisting in a sour look that spoiled his handsome features.

'Well, you know that if I were in charge I'd do things very differently,' he snarled. 'This estate is a millstone around our neck. I'd get rid of it.'

'And destroy five hundred years of our heritage?'

'The trouble with you Ben is that you want to be Lord of the Manor, the benevolent squire,' Tristan sneered. 'But I'm a realist. That's why I gave Rebecca up for dead years ago but you still cling on, spending money, wasting time visiting. What are you trying to do — salve your conscience? You think the guilt will go away? Maybe you ought to go to church after all. You've had a thing about that vicar since the beginning. Pity I got there first.'

Maddy drew in a gasp as Ben shot up out of his chair and Tristan took a step back. But the blow she was expecting didn't come. Instead Ben clenched his fists at his side; all the anger seemed to drain out of him, his expression changing to weary disappointment.

'Go Tristan, just go.'

Tristan nodded.

'You ought to know that I've had meetings with Andrew Kinnerton, my lawyer,' he said. 'He's going to see if he can break this power of attorney. It's not right that you have all the say with father still alive.'

Ben sat down again.

'I'll get the money in the end!' was Tristan's parting shot as he made for the door.

There was nowhere for Maddy to hide. She jumped back as Tristan came storming out. He saw her yet said nothing, passing on his way. She heard the front door slam followed by the roar of a car engine and the scrunch of gravel as he drove away.

Maddy's mind was reeling from what she'd learned about Tristan, but even more from what she'd learned about Ben; he'd wanted her from the beginning? What craziness was that? He was one of the most disagreeable people she'd ever met and his opinion of her appeared to be the same. How could he possibly like her?

She'd just about made up her mind to creep out the way she'd come when the scrape of a chair told her it was too late; Ben was at the door. He pulled up in shock as he saw her there.

'What are you doing here?' his dark eyes flashed at her, almost black with indignation.

'The front door was open, there was no one around. I did knock . . . and then I heard voices . . . ' Maddy made a deliberate attempt to stop rambling. 'I came to speak to you about Lucas Carson's rent but maybe now is not a good time.'

'How much of that conversation did you hear?'

'Enough,' she replied cryptically, then added, 'All of it, actually.'

He stared at her as if he didn't believe her — or at least, as if he didn't want to believe her.

'Listen,' she said, 'I'm sorry. I shouldn't have just walked in. I'll speak to you again. Let me just ask you to please consider Mr Carson. He's about to go out of business.'

She fled the awkward situation then and something told her that Ben Collett-Evans was relieved she'd escaped too.

10

Maddy still couldn't come to terms with what she'd overheard at Collet Hall, the evidence of what Tristan was really like. Had he pursued her only because Ben had expressed an interest? How could she have been so taken in by his charm!

Worryingly she began to wonder if she had a blind spot when it came to judging men. After all, her track record hadn't been particularly good up until now.

'Are you looking forward to the party at Collett Hall?' Ros asked her. She was arranging the church flowers as Maddy popped in to replenish her supplies for taking communion to the housebound.

'What party?'

'Has nobody told you? It's traditional,' Ros snipped the stem of a lily. 'It's been held at the hall for donkeys' years, usually the second Sunday in Advent. All the tenants, parishioners and the hoi-polloi turn up. Malcolm, your predecessor, used to love it.'

'Nobody's told me,' Maddy shook her head. She wondered whether she should go, how awkward it would be; but then she was the vicar and her absence would be noted.

'Ethan's determined to get there on his crutches,' Ros smiled. 'There's usually a children's entertainer and the food is great.' Ros suddenly stopped fussing with the flowers and looked at her keenly. 'Is everything alright?'

Maddy smiled faintly. 'I've just been overhearing things I shouldn't have,' she replied.

'Not Cecil Pugh again!'

'No, not him.'

'That man should be excommunicated. He's a pain in the you-know-what. I've written to the bishop in support of you.'

'Really?' Maddy felt touched.

'Of course. There's no way we want to lose you!'

★ ★ ★

It was Maddy's day off and she wondered what to do. She'd been into Wryton countless times already and really, after two visits there wasn't much else to see. Nor did she fancy driving all the way into the city. And although there were plenty of places of interest to explore in the area she was growing tired of doing it alone; in her previous parish there'd been young professionals around her age and she'd never been short of company. Here in the middle of nowhere it was different. Ros was the only one she could consider a close friend and she was busy with her family on Saturdays.

It was a glorious day, the low sun casting shadows across the lake, the mountains stark against a winter sky. Maddy decided to do what she'd intended to do ever since she'd got permission to walk over Collett-Evans land — explore the perimeter of the lake.

After packing a rucksack she set off in the opposite direction to the grounds of Collett Hall, clambering over styles and squelching through muddy fields, keeping an eye open for wildlife.

On the far side of the lake the path came to an end two hundred yards short of the boating sheds and she was forced to take a detour through the tiny hamlet before cutting down a farm track and rejoining the path at the water's edge.

Here some ramblers were sitting at wooden tables in a picnic area, steam and the aroma of soup rising from their flasks. Maddy exchanged greetings then retreated to her own table — it was her day off and she wanted to be alone.

Across the water she picked out the copse of scotch pines and the grey stone of Saint David's nestling among them. Tucked away behind the church was the vicarage and a little further on, on slightly raised ground, the windows of Collett Hall winked in the midday sunshine. She munched on a tuna sandwich and considered the complications which lay behind its doors.

The ramblers moved on, wishing her good walking. It was nice that they didn't know who she was; there was precious little opportunity to escape recognition in this community.

Soon afterwards, feeling cold, she packed up and set off to walk back home. The ground became more difficult to negotiate as she reached the east end of the lake, marshy and overgrown. When Maddy eventually came to a well maintained fence she knew she'd reached the boundary of Collett Hall. Without a second thought she clambered over and continued on her way, striding out along a delineated path winding its way through rhododendron bushes before petering out on a wide expanse of grass.

She recognised the place — it was where she'd been confronted by Ben Collett-Evans and accused of trespassing the last time. Suddenly she saw him, standing on the jetty. The boat was tied up and he had no fishing rod this time. The dog sat obediently at his side as he stared out across the lake.

Maddy wondered if she could slip past but then he turned.

'I saw you coming,' he said, hands shoved in his pockets.

'Well I was given permission, if you remember.'

He turned away again. This was her chance to pass by and get away from his cool gaze. Maddy didn't. She settled her rucksack more securely on her back and drew up behind him.

'Is this where it happened? The accident with your sister?'

'What do you know of it?' he shot her an accusing glance.

'Only what people say.'

'People talk too much.'

'I suppose they wanted to fill me in as a newcomer and the vicar.'

He said nothing.

'Look, tell me it's none of my business if you like, but you seem to be carrying a heavy burden.'

'And you want me to share it with you? That's what vicar's do I suppose, it's your job isn't it?'

'Even if I wasn't a vicar I'd be concerned.'

He looked ambivalent. Maddy really thought he might be on the point of opening up; then he looked away again, out over the lake, his mouth set in a grim line. It wasn't like Tristan's at all; it didn't have that lazy, sullen turn to it. She found herself wondering when he'd last laughed.

She changed tack, thinking that if she exposed her own frailties it might encourage him to do the same.

'I didn't know that Tristan was like that,' she said. 'The things I overheard the other day, about the money, and the rest of it. He always made out that you were the bad brother.'

'Tristan knows how to charm,' came the wry comment.

'I saw him in Wryton a while back. He was with a woman he seemed to be very intimate with.'

'You weren't the first and you won't be the last,' Ben looked at her again. 'I didn't like the way he was behaving towards you.'

'He saw me as a conquest didn't he?' Maddy said it for him. ''Let's see if I can get the vicar.' I almost got taken in,' she shrugged. 'We all have our weaknesses.'

The rest of what Tristan had said in the heat of the moment hung in the air between them.

'I'd better go,' Maddy said finally.

'I couldn't save her,' Ben suddenly said. 'I tried. I dived in, got her up from the bottom, but it was too late.'

'I'm sure you did everything you could.'

'It wasn't enough,' he frowned.

'Maybe you need to forgive yourself,' Maddy suggested gently. 'I always feel it's a bit presumptuous to hold on to guilt when God has forgiven us. Think about it.'

She continued on her way wondering

what to make of Ben Collett-Evans. This much was certain; his abrasiveness was calculated to hide his pain. And he probably didn't have anything against her personally, it was what she stood for. He reacted violently because he was having a battle with his conscience. She'd seen it before.

★ ★ ★

Chloe was waiting for her when she got back, sitting on the vicarage wall, swinging her legs in an agitated manner. At least I'm forgiven, Maddy thought.

'Hi,' she smiled acting as if Chloe's disaffected departure on Sunday had never happened. 'I've just been for a walk around the lake.'

'I saw you talking to him!' Chloe jerked her head.

For a moment Maddy thought the teenager might have been spying until she explained that she'd rowed across and had been coming in to the jetty by the church when she'd seen them.

'What were you talking about?'

'Just passing pleasantries.'

Chloe looked as if she didn't believe her.

'Can we say evening prayer together?' she asked, letting it go.

Maddy didn't usually bother on her day off but who was she to discourage an enthusiasm for prayer?

'Let me get my keys,' she said.

Chloe waited in the hallway while she deposited her rucksack, then followed her moodily over to the church.

'What do I do about hating them?' she asked as Maddy lit some candles against the afternoon gloom (no need to ask to whom she referred). 'I'm not supposed to hate people; I'm a Christian.'

'I always find that the most effective way to deal with hate is to pray for the person.'

Chloe pulled a face. 'How can I when we're about to lose everything because of them?'

'That's what C S Lewis said,' Maddy sat down in her stall and opened her prayer book. 'You'll find the more you pray for someone the less you dislike them.'

'I can't believe that.'

'You're fourteen Chloe. Don't be too hard on yourself. There's a lot going on in your life at the moment.'

'Maybe I shouldn't even be here,' she half rose from the choir stall opposite. 'The horrible things I think, I want to do . . .'

'That's precisely why you should be!' Maddy said hurriedly. 'Sit down Chloe. Let's pray. I'd rather do it with you than alone. You can lead today if you like.'

They went through the short service of prayers, readings and canticles. Chloe was particularly fervent with no joy in her tone; she sounded troubled.

'Do you want to come to tea?' Maddy asked, snuffing out the candles when they'd finished. She could see her breath hanging in the cold air and was longing

130

for the warmth of central heating.

'I've got to row back before it gets dark.'

'I can drive you home.'

'No!' Chloe said adamantly, shaking her head. Usually she would have jumped at the chance to spend time at the vicarage.

'Is everything alright?' Maddy followed her out into the December afternoon, locking the heavy door behind them.

'I just wanted to say the service. It made me feel better. You're right, prayer helps,' came the toneless reply.

Maddy sniffed the air. Gloom was seeping through the shrubs and trees and creeping over tombstones.

'It's cold and it's getting dark. I don't know whether you should row back,' she said.

'I know this lake like the back of my hand,' Chloe assured her.

'Well be careful. I wouldn't like to think of you having to swim in this freezing water.'

131

'I can't swim,' said Chloe matter of factly and waved before turning down the lane to the water's edge.

Maddy hung back in the shadows until she heard the tell-tale splash of oars in water. As the sound receded she walked down to the shore and watched until the little boat was eventually swallowed up in the descending dusk.

Still she couldn't settle as, back at the vicarage, she unpacked her rucksack and set about preparing tea. She waited an hour before ringing Lucas Carson, not wanting to worry him by calling before Chloe had had a chance to get back.

'She's just come in this instant, Vicar,' he answered her enquiry. 'Didn't even say hello. She's gone straight to her room.'

'That's teenagers for you,' Maddy said lightly.

Even though she felt relieved that Chloe had returned home safely she wondered why it had taken the teenager so long and what she could have been up to since she'd left the church over an hour ago.

★ ★ ★

Maddy was contemplating having a bath when the doorbell rang just after eight-o'clock. She groaned. Who could it be at this time on a Saturday night? Not an emergency, please; not with a full Sunday ahead of her tomorrow.

The person standing waiting in the porch was the last person she expected to see.

'Tristan!'

'May I come in?' he held out a bottle of wine.

'Er, well I was thinking of . . . ' she was going to say bed but didn't think that was somehow appropriate.

'I just want a chance to explain things to you, what you overheard the other day. It's unfinished business, isn't it?'

With a shrug Maddy invited him in.

'I don't feel like drinking,' she said as

she took the wine. 'It's Sunday tomorrow, after all.'

'Keep it then. Enjoy it in your own time. Hmm, cosy,' he said, surveying the sitting room as he took off his dark wool coat and lay it over the back of a chair.

She hadn't bothered to tidy up; there were books and newspapers spread over the coffee table, a pile of bills she'd been meaning to sort through on the floor and socks and tee shirts airing on the radiators.

'What is it you want to say?' she said brusquely.

'You may have misunderstood my conversation with Ben.'

'It sounded like an argument not a conversation.'

'Indeed, yes, Ben is like that, I'm afraid, always very brusque.'

Maddy didn't comment that he was the one who'd appeared to be doing most of the shouting.

'You see, we have different ideas of how to run the estate,' Tristan brushed his trousers as he sat down uninvited on the sofa. 'It's been going downhill for years. I've felt we should shed some of our liabilities, sell off land, invest in property and the stock market — my father thought it was a good idea too. Then he got sick and we both lost control as Ben acquired power of attorney. Now we have to do things his way.'

'Didn't he say your investments have never made money?'

'Some you lose. But you make it back given time and fresh injections of cash. Ben is just too blinkered to see that.'

She would have believed Tristan before; before she'd seen him with another woman in Wryton, before she'd heard his tirade against his brother, before she'd seen the desolation in Ben's soul and heard the guilt in his words this afternoon. For all Tristan's charm and Ben's curtness she felt she knew which was the more reliable brother.

Tristan must have seen the ambivalence in her eyes for he said with a smile that only just barely covered the intensity in his voice: 'He makes things up about me!'

'He could hardly have known he had an audience the other day,' Maddy retorted. 'Anyway if that's true he's not the only one; why did you tell me your sister was dead?'

He looked taken aback. 'I didn't think it important,' he shrugged. 'She's as good as anyway.'

Maddy told him about her discovery at the hospital although she didn't say how angry Ben had been when he'd found her with Rebecca.

'Are you ashamed of her?' she challenged.

'No, I'm just not going to waste my energy on a situation that can't be changed. Ben can spend his life feeling guilty because he failed if he wants, but I'm not going to. Isn't that what the church teaches — forgive, forget, move on?'

'Not in that way.' Maddy's breath was taken away by his callous indifference. She hadn't sat down the whole time, standing in front of the wood burning stove. Now Tristan rose from the sofa.

'Now, Vicar, you are determined to think the worst of me, and we were getting on so well. Have you been put off by what I said about Ben liking you? It was just my little dig at him,' his voice was smooth as butter as he moved towards her.

'Actually I was put off by what I saw in The Duke the other week.'

That stopped him in his tracks. He frowned.

'You and the blonde woman. You seemed very intimate judging by the kiss. And what was it you said? 'Nothing's been happening here; I'm glad you're back, liven up this dull place a bit.''

'She's just a friend,' the affable smile returned.

Maddy raised an eyebrow.

'I find you much more interesting.'

She couldn't believe it; he was still making a play for her despite having been rumbled! It was as if he needed to prove he could have anyone if he put his mind to it.

'It's just a game for you isn't it, Tristan?' she stepped aside. Her heart began to race. She was alone in the house with this man. How well did she really know him? Underneath the charming exterior he'd shown that he was capable of great anger.

'I've never been with a vicar before. As I say, I find that interesting.'

'And I'm not a fool. I'd like you to go now please.'

'Are you sure about that?'

'Quite.'

She stood her ground, refusing to look intimidated. He chewed his lip as if he was trying to make up his mind what to do. Then he turned away quickly and sharply.

'Your loss,' he said, catching up his coat from the back of the chair. 'I'll see myself out.'

Maddy breathed a sigh of relief as she heard the door slam behind him.

She waited until the angry roar of a car engine and the screech of tyres said he'd really gone. Then she picked up the bottle of wine from the coffee table and looked at it — not your cheap plonk from the supermarket. Well, however expensive it was it would be going onto the bottle stall at the next parish fundraising event. She wanted nothing more from Tristan Collett-Evans.

11

The party started at three-o'clock before dusk fell. Maddy decided to walk just in case she drank too much. Through the hedges edging the lane she could see lights and lanterns strung out among the trees in the grounds of Collett Hall already glowing in rich reds and oranges against the gloom of the afternoon.

The driveway leading up to the house was full of cars, some parked on the grass verge. Ken and Glenda Williams waved to her as they were getting out of theirs.

'Afternoon vicar. Not a bad day for it,' Ken greeted her.

And it wasn't. It hadn't rained and the clouds were clearing to promise a frosty night. In front of the house the area was full of expensive cars.

'Looks like the Lord Lieutenant is here,' Glenda commented.

'There's Sir Aubrey Whettleton,' Ken nodded in the direction of an elegant white haired man climbing the steps to the main entrance.

'Aye, and Cecil is there right on cue.'

Maddy saw her least favourite person in the parish obsequiously shaking the hand of Sir Aubrey and ushering him inside.

She should have anticipated that the family would have the best connections. She didn't expect to see the bishop though. Bishop Wyn stood before the fire in the sitting room, a glass of something alcoholic in his hand, conversing with a middle-aged impressive looking couple. She could hear his rich, clear enunciation from across the room and it left her cold as she recalled her interview with him a few weeks ago.

He spared her a glance and nodded. There was no way Maddy was going to interrupt.

She began to mingle. Only three months in the parish and already she knew so many people and felt a part of the life of Llyn Ddu. Ros was there with Tim and the boys, Ethan seated near a table heaving with food, lapping up the attention from concerned adults while his brother pulled faces at his side.

Even Lucas Carson had come which she thought was incredibly magnanimous of him considering the Collett-Evans were the source of his financial worries. She went up to him and said so.

'It's just business,' he shrugged. 'We all have to make ends meet.'

Maddy wondered how he could be so forgiving. No, resigned was the word; it was as if the fight had gone out of him.

'Is Chloe with you?' she asked.

'She's around somewhere.'

Maddy decided to look for her. Negotiating her way through the crowds she suddenly found herself face to face with Tristan. For a moment neither of them knew what to say.

'How are you Tristan?' Maddy broke the silence.

'Fine.' There was none of that

courting warmth in his voice. Now she'd seen him in his true colours she realised the piercing blue eyes were cold, not sparkling, and the affability which appeared to draw people in was really a shield. Everything was superficial, a deception.

'Nice party,' she said.

The woman she'd seen with him at The Duke a couple of weeks ago appeared at his side.

'Tris darling,' she grabbed his arm and looked daggers at Maddy. 'Who's this?' adding as her gaze alighted on Maddy's clerical collar. 'Oh, the vicar, a woman. How quaint.'

The woman was obviously ignorant of her short history with Tristan.

'I'm Maddy,' she introduced herself.

'Charlotte. Pleased to meet you. Now, please don't think you can persuade Tristan into church,' she laughed. 'He's a lost cause.'

'Yes, I rather think he is,' Maddy delivered a withering look before passing on by.

Even though she knew what he was she hated being played for a fool. It still hurt. It reminded her of Michael's betrayal and all the old hurts came flooding to the surface again, the ones she thought she'd buried in the past few months.

To counteract the feelings she went back into the morning room and piled a plate full of food, stuffing herself with smoked salmon and dips. Through the open doors she saw Chloe, dressed in a bright scarlet dress, sitting on one of the window seats in the hall. She was chatting with a boy. Good sign, Maddy thought, except Chloe looked distracted, constantly looking away from him to the view beyond the window.

Now was not the time to speak with her, not if there was a boy around — not impressive having the local vicar as your friend.

Maddy wondered where Ben Collett-Evans was. Not that she was interested in him, but this was his party after all and the host should be present. She was still stuffing her face when she saw Bishop Wyn approaching. Quickly she put her plate down and wiped her fingers on a serviette. He looked at her as if he didn't know whether to be pleased or not. Maddy was expecting another barbed comment or warning. Instead he said, 'It seems you're very popular in the parish Miss Green. I've had a number of your congregation approach me informing me that they are happy with you so far.'

'Oh, really, that's kind,' Maddy felt stunned at the good news.

'There's still the matter of quota payments of course,' he reminded her. 'Every parish has to make its contribution.'

'We will.'

'Yes,' he said snootily, looking her up and down. 'Well if you're really in trouble the diocese has an emergency fund to help you out; you can apply to that.' It sounded as if he were loath to impart the information. 'It is the last resort of course . . . '

'Thank you.'

Maddy was wondering how she was going to extricate herself from the conversation — she was certain she had food at the corner of her mouth because the bishop's gaze of distaste kept being drawn to it — when a teenager's agitated voice drew their attention. Chloe!

Maddy hurried to the doorway. The crowd had gone quiet with astonishment. Maddy groaned. Ben Collett-Evans had made an appearance at last and Chloe had cornered him. Her face was red with indignation and she was on the point of tears.

'Who do you think you are?' she jabbed her finger at him. 'Because of you my dad's going to lose his business. We're going to lose our home. Where do you think we're going to go?'

Ben looked as if he might apologise, his hands raised in a placatory manner, but Chloe didn't give him a chance.

'Just because you've got a big house and can throw your money around with a party you think you can push us around. Remember Letty Pendle. One day you'll get your comeuppance!'

Maddy saw Lucas Carson pushing through the crowd.

'Chloe, what do you think you're doing? Come away at once,' he grabbed her arm. 'I'm sorry Mr Collett-Evans.'

'No, I won't come away!' she shook off her father's grip. 'It's not fair. We're going to lose everything, Dad. Don't you care? Haven't we lost enough already? How can you be so nice to him?'

Lucas Carson lunged for his daughter again, but Chloe was too quick for him and stormed off, the crowd parting to let her through.

'Let her go Lucas,' somebody said. 'She'll calm down on her own.'

'She'd better apologise when she does,' Lucas Carson fumed.

Ben laid a hand on his shoulder, consoling and understanding.

'Don't worry about it Mr Carson, it'll be alright.'

And despite his polite words, Lucas Carson shook off the hand in a gesture that told how he really felt about the situation.

Maddy didn't wait to see what happened next. Something told her she should go after Chloe.

She did not appear to be in the house. By chance Maddy glanced out of a window and saw a lone figure hurrying down the lawn towards the lake, her red dress bright against the gloom of the afternoon. Instinct told her to follow. Chloe had no coat on for one thing and the winter's day was cold.

'Chloe!' she cried out as she ran over the lawn. 'Chloe, wait!'

Chloe didn't look back. If anything she seemed to speed up. By the time Maddy arrived breathless at the water's edge Chloe had untied the boat at the jetty and rowed out about fifty yards from the shore.

'Chloe, what are you doing? Come back. If you want to go home I'll drive you. It's getting dark. Come on, for goodness' sake.'

The teenager showed no sign of having heard her. Maddy's heart began to race as Chloe stood up in the rowing boat making it rock.

'Chloe!'

Quite deliberately the teenager tipped herself over the edge and into the icy water. *I can't swim*, Maddy remembered the last words Chloe had spoken to her.

'Chloe!' she screamed again as she ran onto the jetty to see the youngster thrashing about in the dark water.

Before she could think of jumping in herself — she was not the world's best swimmer — someone ran past her in a rush of air and launched themselves into the lake. Ben, it was Ben!

She watched him striking out with powerful strokes. A gaggle of geese burst out of the reeds, the flap of their wings and cries of protests mingling with the screams of Chloe. Quickly Maddy fished her mobile out of her pocket and rang for an ambulance.

'What's happening? Oh my god, who's gone into the lake?' Maddy looked around to see Ros at her side.

'It's Chloe,' she said urgently. 'Ben's gone in after her. I've called an ambulance. We're going to need some blankets.'

'I'll do it,' said Ros setting off at a sprint back up to the house.

With a sigh of relief Maddy saw that Ben had reached the flailing teenager. It took him a while to get her under control and then he was swimming for the shore with her chin cupped in his hand.

Maddy knelt down at the jetty's edge, reaching out for Chloe as Ben brought her in.

'Take her,' he spluttered, pushing her up out of the water.

Maddy helped her out onto the slick wood where Chloe coughed and gasped and shivered. She was covered in slime and algae, water from her hair running in rivulets down her face.

'Chloe, Chloe, are you alright? You crazy girl!' Maddy wrapped comforting arms around her and rocked her.

'I . . . I meant to do it Saturday, after we did the service together,' she choked. 'But I chickened out. And today, as soon as I went into the water I knew I didn't want to die but it was too late. I couldn't swim,' sobs racked her thin body.

'It's alright, Ben rescued you,' Maddy glanced up at him as he heaved himself up onto the jetty. He looked all in.

A crowd of party guests were suddenly swarming around them, Lucas Carson the first in line.

'Baby, baby, what happened?'

'Daddy.' Shakily Chloe got up and fell into his arms.

'Here,' Ros threw a blanket around her shivering shoulders.

'An accident,' Maddy explained. 'Chloe was in the boat and it tipped her into the water.'

'My God, she can't swim!' Lucas Carson hugged his daughter close.

'Luckily Mr Collett-Evans dived in and saved her,' she looked at Ben who was slowly getting to his feet. He looked dazed.

'Mr Collett-Evans, I don't know what to say. I don't know how to thank you,' Lucas Carson extended a hand.

'Anyone would have done it,' Ben nodded.

Maddy sensed that he wanted to shrink into the surrounding bushes, to disappear, but everyone was looking at him in awe and applauding.

'My brother the hero,' said Tristan coming forward, but there was an edge to his voice. He clapped Ben on the back and because Maddy was standing so close she heard the almost whispered words said with a false cameraderie, 'Managed it this time, then?'

She saw Ben flinch and wondered if anyone else had seen it too. It was time to move everyone away.

'I've called an ambulance,' she announced. 'We'd better get these water rats back to the house!'

Nobody stopped Maddy as she went upstairs later, looking into the rooms leading off the landing until she finally came to one that was ajar and knocked lightly before entering. Ben Collett-Evans was sitting on the edge of the bed, staring into space. She could see he'd showered and changed into fresh clothes, his wet hair dripping about his shoulders.

He looked up as she came in and didn't think it strange that the vicar should suddenly appear in his bedroom.

'How is she?' he asked.

'The paramedics have just finished checking her out; she won't need to go to hospital. Thankfully she didn't sustain any injuries. Her dad's taking her home now. How are you?'

'Better now I've showered.'

'No, I didn't mean that,' Maddy came closer. She expected him to snap at her intrusion but he didn't. 'That was a brave thing you did.'

'Anyone would have done the same.'

But all Maddy could think of was her moment of hesitation, considering the coldness of the water, how far out Chloe was and the fact that she was only a mediocre swimmer.

'If I'd gone in,' she said, 'she would have pulled me under. I wouldn't have had the strength to to be able to save her. Why were you there so quickly?'

'I saw you run out,' he said. 'I saw the girl going down to the lake and after our confrontation I could see she was upset. It was an instinctive reaction, I suppose.'

Boldly she sat on the bed at his side.

'I heard what Tristan said. It was cruel.'

'That's Tris for you,' Ben shrugged.

Maddy swallowed before deciding to take the plunge.

'What happened with your sister?'

Ben examined his hands then sighed deeply.

'She and her friends took a picnic out on to the lake. They were messing around, the boat tipped over. Rebecca

154

must have knocked her head against the side as she went into the water,' he grimaced as the memories came back. 'I was out walking Hab, I saw it happen. They were further out than today. She sank to the bottom, got tangled up in the weeds. By the time I'd got there I was too late. I dived and dived and kept diving . . . ' he trailed off.

'It wasn't your fault. You did everything you could.'

'It wasn't enough. They took her to hospital and put her on life support; she's been in a coma ever since. Once our father had lost the apple of his eye his mental decline accelerated. This was not a happy place to be any more.'

Instinctively Maddy placed a reassuring hand on his arm.

'You know that you saved Chloe's life today, and if it had been humanly possible you would have saved your sister too, I know it.'

There was hunger for redemption in his dark eyes as he looked at her.

'Sometimes things happen and there seems to be no rhyme or reason,' Maddy said. 'Today should have shown you one thing at least — that you're a good person.'

'Do you know why I withdrew the family contribution to the parish?'

Maddy shook her head.

'Because it seemed hypocritical. We never attend. Tristan is . . . well, Tristan is what he is. And I've lost any faith I have because of what happened. I wanted to find it again but didn't think I was worthy.'

Maddy opened her mouth to speak but he continued, 'I've been thinking about what you said the other day, about the presumption of not being able to forgive myself.'

'We're all imperfect Ben.' It was the first time she'd addressed him by his Christian name. 'I mean, who am I to be a vicar?'

She saw the ghost of a smile at the corner of his mouth.

'You're probably a very good one. At

least you care about people. You're the one who went after Chloe. And you haven't stopped badgering me about her father!'

'Yes, about that . . . '

He chuckled.

'You're a good person,' she told him again.

Then before she had time to register what was happening he'd leaned in and kissed her. Maddy supposed she should have been shocked, but she wasn't. Despite the stand-offs, his rudeness and their differences of opinion it seemed right somehow, as if she'd come home.

'That was presumptuous too,' he said as they drew apart. 'I wasn't intending to, I mean . . . '

Maddy smiled.

'Sometimes presumption is allowed.' And this time she leaned across and kissed him.

12

Maddy called on the Carsons first thing the following morning. 'Welcome vicar,' Lucas Carson beamed as he opened the door. 'Chloe's here. I thought she should have a day off school after yesterday's scare.'

The teenager was sitting on the sofa, wrapped up in a blanket and watching TV. She quickly turned it off as Maddy entered the caravan.

'How are you feeling?'

'Much better.'

She was certainly looking less miserable Maddy thought, but surviving a brush with death tended to have that effect.

'We can't thank Mr Collett-Evans enough,' he said now, indicating that Maddy should sit down in the only armchair while he perched on the arm of the sofa at his daughter's side. 'If he hadn't been there . . . ' he shook his head. 'I knew Chloe was unhappy, what with the divorce and the uncertainty about the business.' The rest was left unsaid as he gave Chloe a hug and kissed the top of her head. Whatever Chloe had said about the event, whatever Maddy had said about it being an accident, he was aware of the undercurrents. 'And thank you to you, vicar.'

'Maddy.'

'Maddy. For taking an interest in Chloe and encouraging her. She speaks very highly of you.'

Maddy smiled.

'Mrs Lannigan — Ros — has invited me over to tea,' Chloe said. 'She said she'll teach me how to make pottery too if I'm interested.'

'That's a brilliant idea,' Maddy enthused, glad that Ros was taking on the suggestion that she might be a mother figure to the teenager.

'But the best news is . . . ' Chloe looked up at her beaming father.

'I had a phone call from Mr Collett-Evans earlier this morning,' Lucas Carson said. 'He couldn't get a word in edgeways at first I was so grateful for what he did yesterday. He said he's not putting up the ground rent on the business and the caravan.'

'Oh that's wonderful!'

'And, not only that, but he wants to see me this afternoon, says he wants to talk about employing me during the winter months.'

'Perhaps the Collett-Evans aren't all bad,' Chloe admitted.

'Well you know, he's had his own demons to contend with,' Maddy defended him. 'I didn't like him at first either, but now . . . '

He wasn't a heartless mercenary after all. Her heart sang.

Lucas made tea for them all and Maddy stayed a while, talking about their Christmas plans. At least the Carsons had some hope now, a festive season to look forward to.

'Will you be alright for the youth

service on Sunday night?' Maddy reminded Chloe as she was leaving. 'I'm relying on you. You're my star!'

'Of course I'll be there.'

As she left, a warmth in her heart that couldn't be affected by the grey, bitter wind, she thought of Ben. Should she get in touch with him, use the Carsons' news as a pretext? No, there would be no chasing. He needed time to sort himself out.

★ ★ ★

There was one more parish council meeting before Christmas. When Maddy walked into the church hall it was buzzing with conversations about the events of the previous Sunday and Cecil Pugh looked out of sorts. And well he might, for she'd received an official letter from the Collett-Evans' solicitors informing her that the family contribution to parish funds was to be re-instated. No doubt Cecil, as treasurer, would have had the same letter.

She brought the meeting to order.

'May we say first of all vicar how proud we are of you,' Ken Williams said. 'If you hadn't been looking out for Chloe Carson no one would have noticed her going down to the lake and the poor child would most probably have drowned.'

Once again Maddy confessed her reluctance to jump into the water.

'It was Ben Collett-Evans who saved her,' she reminded them.

'But you played a major part, don't be modest,' Ken wagged a chiding finger at her.

Cecil Pugh looked as if he were sucking lemons. She decided to give them all the good news about the re-instated money. It was met with cheers and applause.

'So it seems you do have the right powers of persuasion,' Maisie said, looking pointedly at Cecil.

'Now that really was nothing to do with me,' Maddy smiled. 'Let's just say God moves in a mysterious way.'

'So he does and maybe he's sent you to us for a reason,' Ken said with authority as he suddenly stood up and surveyed them all. 'I know what's been happening: letters to the bishop, grumbles, people trying to undermine what the vicar is doing. Well I for one am very happy with her, lots of people are. She's not going away, are you?' he turned to her and Maddy shook her head. 'So let's all pull together and work to make great things happen.'

The whole gathering, apart from a couple of people, clapped. After the meeting had ended Maddy sought out Cecil Pugh.

'Listen Cecil,' she said briskly for it was time to come straight to the point. 'I would like us to work together. If you find you can't then maybe you ought to resign as treasurer.'

He looked appalled. She knew what his response would be — he didn't want to lose the position which gave him influence in the church.

'I have my conscience,' he said stiffly.

'Fine. Maybe it's time for you to resign.'

'No.'

'Then work with me. We'll have our differences of opinion, no doubt, but I can live with that if you can.'

He studied her through narrowed eyes, then nodded, curtly, like an army sergeant receiving orders.

'I'll carry on.'

'Good.'

That was all she was going to get for now, but as she exchanged a glance with Ken she knew that the rest of her council were going to keep him in order.

★ ★ ★

The church was packed on that winter's afternoon nine days before Christmas. The musicians and singers had squeezed themselves into the space by the pulpit and the first two rows were occupied by the children and teenagers taking part in the service. Even Ethan had turned up on crutches, determined to do his reading.

'It's years since we've had so many young people in church,' Maddy overheard Anita Wilson say to her friend. Her heart glowed with pride.

She took her place at the end of the front pew and allowed the service to happen. Chloe had made an excellent job of directing and seemed to grow in confidence as she led the service.

At one point Maddy turned around and drew in a gasp — Ben was sitting three rows back on the other side of the aisle. She could hardly believe that he'd come. When it was all over she began to mingle with the congregation, shaking hands vigorously as people showered her with compliments.

'Nothing to do with me,' she said. 'It was Chloe Carson who did all the hard work.'

And when she glanced across to Ben she could see Chloe catching his arm, her face aglow. It seemed the teenager had reached a turning point, and maybe

Ben Collett-Evans had too.

Eventually they managed to work their way towards each other.

'That really was a lovely service,' he said, extending a hand. Maddy smiled at the formality.

'Thank you for what you've done for Lucas Carson,' she said.

'I thought about it and you were right.'

'Tristan didn't come with you?' Maddy looked around.

'He's gone back to London. He hasn't given up on trying to overturn the power of attorney but,' Ben shrugged, 'I've decided not to worry about that. There are more important things.'

He looked up the chancel towards the window of Christ in glory, now black and opaque as the night drew in.

'How does it feel to be back?' Maddy asked softly.

For a long moment he didn't speak, considering her with warm, deep brown eyes.

166

'There is a place for you here.'

He smiled. 'I'm beginning to believe that now.'

And as she looked around at the faces which had become so familiar, at the winking lights on the Christmas tree, the flickering candlelight burnishing bronze and silver, but particularly as she looked at Ben Collett-Evans, Maddy felt she'd truly found her place too.

THE END

We do hope that you have enjoyed reading this large print book.

Did you know that all of our titles are available for purchase?

We publish a wide range of high quality large print books including:
Romances, Mysteries, Classics
General Fiction
Non Fiction and Westerns

Special interest titles available in large print are:
The Little Oxford Dictionary
Music Book, Song Book
Hymn Book, Service Book

Also available from us courtesy of Oxford University Press:
Young Readers' Dictionary
(large print edition)
Young Readers' Thesaurus
(large print edition)

For further information or a free brochure, please contact us at:
Ulverscroft Large Print Books Ltd.,
The Green, Bradgate Road, Anstey,
Leicester, LE7 7FU, England.
Tel: (00 44) **0116 236 4325**
Fax: (00 44) **0116 234 0205**

Other titles in the
Linford Romance Library:

FOLLOW YOUR HEART

Margaret Mounsdon

Marie Stanford's life is turned upside down when she is asked to house sit for her mysterious Aunt Angela, who has purchased a converted barn property in the Cotswolds. Nothing is as it seems . . . Who is the mysterious Jed Soames and why is he so interested in Maynard's? And can she trust Pierre Dubois, Aunt Angela's stepson? Until Marie can find the answers to these questions she dare not let herself follow her heart.

A LOVE WORTH WAITING FOR

Karen Abbott

In the lovely village of Manorbier in Pembrokeshire, Jasmine gets the opportunity to open up a teashop — her dream come true. However, disturbing events threaten her business prospects, forcing Jasmine to search her heart and discover who wants the teashop closed. Is it the controlling boyfriend she has put in the past? Or someone wanting the premises for himself . . . local artist Rhys Morgan, for instance? Jasmine has to put her heart on hold until the sinister campaign is over.